PRAISE FOR JILL KNAPP

"Searching for a new Carrie Bradshaw who's on the hunt for her very own Mr. Darcy? You will want to curl up with What Happens To Men When They Move To Manhattan and fall in love all over again. With men, Manhattan and yourself."
– *Shiri Appleby, Actress, HBO's Girls*

"A subtly addicting, fun, and fast-paced story about the realty of twenty-something dating in NYC."
– *Courtney Hamilton, Author of Almost Royalty.*

"A fast-paced, roller-coaster ride through the giddy peaks and Death Valleys of dating in your twenties in the big city, looking for love, and finding yourself."
– *Phoebe Fox, Author of The Break-Up Doctor*

"For any woman who has ever ch——————————————selves... this book is for you."
– *Mandy Hale, Creator*

"...Knapp's book combines love —————————— within the borders of one of t———————————— cities in the world, New York City. But what's most interesting is how the characters find solace in the noise, find happiness in the chaos, and find love in the unique."
– *Kate Avino, The Huffington Post and CEO of Her Culture magazine.*

"A fun and enjoyable read about a young woman in search of her happily ever after. Take it to the beach or snuggle up in bed and dig in."
– *Emily Liebert, award-winning author of You Knew Me When and When We Fall*

JILL KNAPP

I'm currently a blogger for The Huffington Post, and a former college professor. What Happens to Men When They Move to Manhattan? is my debut novel, and the first in a series of books I am writing about being young, single, and living in New York City. I am a native New Yorker, but currently reside in Raleigh, North Carolina. You can follow me on Twitter @JL_Knapp

WHAT HAPPENS TO MEN WHEN THEY MOVE TO MANHATTAN?

JILL KNAPP

Harper impulse
we've got the love

Harper*Impulse* an imprint of
HarperCollins*Publishers Ltd*
77–85 Fulham Palace Road
Hammersmith, London W6 8JB

www.harpercollins.co.uk

A Paperback Original 2014

First published in Great Britain in ebook format by Harper*Impulse* 2014

A catalogue record for this book
is available from the British Library

ISBN: 9780008104993

Automatically produced by Atomik ePublisher from Easypress

To all the city girls …

What Happens to Men When They Move to Manhattan?

"The true New Yorker secretly believes that people living anywhere else have to be, in some sense, kidding." – John Updike

Chapter 1

Good morning, New York

There I was, in the heart of it all. I had finally made it to my dream city.

Living on my own, in my first apartment, had accelerated my formerly conventional social life. Sure, going away to college and living in a dorm had its advantages; first time living away from my overly strict parents, no curfew with the car, and of course the ability to invite a guy over without a twenty-minute-long inquisition from my family.

My father had even composed a "test" to give to all of my dates upon first meeting them. The assessment consisted of around fifty questions, ranging from small queries like name and date of birth, to more invasive interrogation like yearly income, to topical polling such as political and religious ideologies. There was even a separate form to fill out your driver's license and social security numbers. I'll never forget how he handed a freshly printed version to my boyfriend Nicholas the first time he came over my house. Nick had turned to me and said, "Is this for real?" I just shook my head and walked out of the room.

Needless to say, I needed my independence.

Even with all of the freedom college provided, I still lived within the strict and unforgiving guidelines I had always compressed myself into. For as long as I could remember, I believed that if you didn't cheat, lie, or steal, and if you ate all of your veggies and took your vitamins, the world somehow owed you something.

After only three months of living in New York City, to pursue a Master's Degree at NYU, I learned that was, in fact, not the case.

I considered myself lucky, being able to live in an apartment this nice. The deep-mahogany floors, paired with the brand-new appliances in the kitchen were the envy of every young New Yorker south of 23rd Street. This is not how a newcomer is supposed to live. A newly appointed Manhattan-ite should live in a dingy studio apartment up on East 105th Street, or share a confined two-bedroom place with four or five roommates down in Chinatown. No, a new-to-the-town, twenty-two year-old girl, would not normally have the privilege of a washer and dryer in the building, and perish the thought – enough closet space to fit nearly all of her clothing.

Nick's apartment, on the other hand, was anything but pristine. It was located further downtown on the Lower East Side. Sandwiched in between a bodega and beat-up old park, Nick's apartment building was old, bleak, and proverbially falling apart. I felt a pang of guilt over how difficult it must be to live somewhere like that, and how he hadn't had the option of taking out extra student loans to put toward rent like I did. He never seemed to mind, though; said it built "character".

My new life, however, in this very spacious and immaculate West Village apartment had made me into a caricature of myself. Being that I was twenty-two, and living in the greatest city on earth, I took every chance I could get to go out and improve my social life, which unfortunately included improving my alcohol tolerance.

Today, on this blurry autumn morning, I awoke with not only the usual Monday morning hangover, but also an intense burning feeling in my throat. It got worse every time I swallowed, and finished itself off with a dry and uncontrollable cough.

"Damn," I said aloud, to no one in particular. I let out a yawn and then allowed myself a wide stretch in my tiny, twin-sized bed. I squinted at the clock on my bedside table, and uttered a low groan.

I considered going back to sleep, but after hitting the snooze twice already, I knew I had to get out of bed. Even though my time window for showering today had passed, I still had to make myself look presentable and walk to class.

I slowly walked out of my bedroom, passed my roommates' room (the two of them shared the larger, master bedroom), and stumbled feverishly into my kitchen. Exhausted from my journey, I put my head in my hands and leaned over the counter top. The flawless sparkle in the grain of the brand-new, deep-green granite made a mockery of me. The stone was so shiny that if I stared hard enough, I could make out a blurred, reflected version of my face. I knew I couldn't afford this apartment. I had justified this relocation from my parent's suburban home by telling myself that when I was finished with school, I would be making so much money that my student loans would be a thing of the past in no time. I pushed myself off of the granite and figured it was about time to make good on that promise.

My self-loathing was interrupted by the unmistakable clanking of my roommate's heels.

"Good morning," Christina beamed, as she reached right over me and grabbed the last apple.

Christina was one of those girls who were naturally gorgeous, even when she'd just woken up. In my hung-over, and quickly accelerating sick state I was extra aware, and disgusted, by how bright-eyed and effortless she looked. Not to mention she had already showered and was heading out the door while I was running twenty minutes late. We usually woke up around the same time to get ready to go to class and I couldn't find the energy to fight her for the first shower today.

"Is there coffee?" was all I could muster up, as I fumbled around the fridge for bottled water. I yawned again and rubbed my eyes, leaning on the counter for support.

Before she could answer me, I noticed the time and frantically ran into my bedroom to get dressed for class, nearly taking Christina out in the process. I had realized early in the semester that this was not the class to be late to. The professor was a notorious hard ass and had actually called out my friend Olivia for checking the time on her cell phone last week, embarrassing her in front of the entire cohort. Scarred by the memory, I quickly ran a brush through my hair while simultaneously applying my foundation. A few minutes later, I was good to go (well, good enough).

I grabbed my purse and yelled "Bye!" to no one in particular, slamming the door behind me. As soon as I got into the elevator, my phone vibrated. I grabbed it from my purse, desperately hoping it was one of my friends telling me class was cancelled, but instead it was a text message from my boyfriend Nicholas.

It read, "Can't wait 2 C U tomorrow honey, I'm counting down hrs!"

I dropped the phone back into my bag and exited the elevator on the ground floor. I started feeling a quick pang of guilt for ignoring the text, but Nicholas would understand how busy I was and I would re-cap my day with him, in full detail tonight, on the phone. It was comforting to know I could go about my day without having to check in with anyone twenty times, and that he had his own life too. Not to mention we had an undeniable chemistry between us that seemed to have stood the test of time. Or at least the past couple of years. I smiled to myself as I pictured his wide, soulful eyes, his ever-present second-day stubble (which I always referred to as, Oops! I didn't realize I'm so sexy, stubble) and his strong, well-toned arms that just always managed to keep their firmness, no matter how many times he missed the gym. Combine all of that with my favorite thing he did, the way he traced my lips with his finger right before he was about to kiss me, and I was convinced I was in a perfect relationship. I let out a breathy sigh and let the warmth wash over me as I thought about how lucky I was to have such a great guy in my life. Sexy, caring, and smart. What more could you ask for?

Thunder cracking above my head interrupted this solitary pleasant thought. When I got outside I was greeted by a blanket of humid rain and I had, of course, left my umbrella upstairs. I glanced back at the elevator doors that were quickly closing. Since I lived on 18th floor of my apartment building, I rationalized that I had already gone too far to turn around and made my way to 6th Avenue in the pouring rain.

My sneakers did nothing to protect me against the river-sized potholes littering the streets of New York. Each passing minute was more disgusting than the last as I told myself I was going to be sitting with wet socks for the next two hours.

By the time I got to the school, I was drenched and feeling even more morose than when I had woken up. I darted into the ladies' room to use the hand dryer to dry off at least to a comfortable level. When I opened the door, I sighed. There was a line of two girls in front of me, ignoring my soaked state, and gabbing on about having drinks at Crocodile Lounge later tonight. I started to shiver and one of them gave me an uncomfortable side-look. They finally decided to leave and I bent down to fit under the small, inefficient dryer. Feeling a little homeless, I flipped my head over, figuring my hair was the most important thing to get try. Then I reached down, pulled off my sneakers, and let the hot air run over my argyle socks. It was pointless, those babies were done for. I tossed them in the trash, deciding I'd be more comfortable without them.

Two more girls walked into the bathroom, heading straight to the mirrors. I recognized them, but not enough to say hi and start small-talk. Definitely not while I was looking like a drowned rat. After a few more minutes under the hand dryer, I ran my fingers through my puffed-up curls to help smooth them down. Reaching into my purse, I opted for a quick refreshing slick of clear lip-gloss, and a smudge of black eye-liner for good measure. I thought I looked normal enough to start my day.

While I was in the process of giving myself a mini make-over,

I overheard the two girls talking about how difficult they were finding this semester. They were conversing in a loud whisper, but with rapid speech. The brunette with the secretary glasses looked as if she was going to burst into tears at any moment, the red-head with the expensive shoes sympathetically rubbing her back. They both let out a sigh, and then made each other swear they wouldn't tell anyone else, out of fear of seeming weak. I shrugged and collecting my belongings off the sink basin. The girls seemed normal enough, but maybe that was the problem. Maybe you had to be cold and overly-determined to survive here. I shivered both at the thought, and from my clinging wet clothes.

They exited the bathroom, and finally I was alone. I grimaced while silently sympathizing with their pain, making a mental note that I wasn't the only one suffering this year. Turning to the mirror, I allowed myself to stare a few seconds longer, then shook my head and made my way out into the hall.

As I walked down the long, tiled hallway toward my classroom, I felt a memory hit me out of nowhere. I remembered Nick and I, hands intertwined, walking across campus at Rutgers. The sun was shining as we lightly strolled across the pavement. He was anxious for me to meet his friends for the first time; he kept apologizing for how they would inevitably embarrass him. I could still hear the birds chirping on that unusually warm April day. I had stopped walking for a moment, waiting for a gaggle of sorority girls to pass us, and then brushed a strand of brown hair from his face.

"Stop being so nervous," I said, rubbing his hand in mine. "Everything's going to go great. We'll eat, we'll bond, we'll crack jokes at your expense. How bad could it be?"

Nick offered me a laugh and sheepishly looked at the floor. I thought it was sweet, how much he cared about his friends and me getting along. That was the moment I knew I was in love with him.

The sound of a guy cursing at his cellphone broke me out of my daydream, and I quickly remembered where I was. I took a deep breath and opened the large brown door to my lecture hall.

I gingerly walked into the classroom hoping no one would notice my disheveled appearance, and took a quick glance around the room. The class was already going on, but thankfully my friend Michael had saved a seat for me. I breathed a sigh of relief and tried to smooth a deep wrinkle out of my shirt. He turned around slightly and gave me a subtle nod. I nodded back, and then quickly ran my fingers through my hair, attempting to further tame the nest of rain-soaked curls. It was no use; I'd have to sport this Bette Midler from the 80s look for the rest of this class.

I had met Michael only two or three months ago, when school started; it was getting harder to keep track. He and I were in every single class together, which wasn't unusual given that our program in Biology and Behavioral Science only had forty students in it. This meant quick bonding but also steep competition. It kind of reminded me of how you'd make close friendships in summer camp, but then completely forget to call the person come October.

Michael and I had become fast friends after he referenced an old B movie, which just so happened to be one of my favorite films, during the third day of classes. I felt an instant connection that moment, which was a little out of character for me. I usually had a hard time opening up to people. After a good laugh, he composed himself and formally stuck out his hand.

"Michael Rathbourne," he said with a warm smile and perfectly straight teeth. "And you are?"

His confidence had left me a little intimidated. Apart from going on a job interview, I had never formally introduced myself with a handshake before. I studied Michael as he held his warm smile. I couldn't help but notice his full lips and dark-brown eyes, with tiny specs of gold if you looked closely enough. He was dressed well, wearing what looked like an expensive button-down and designer jeans.

"Amalia Hastings," I said, trying my best to sound as confident as he had. I could feel my voice crack as I uttered the last syllable of my name. I squared my shoulders a bit and smiled.

"Well, Amalia Hastings," he repeated my name, still holding my hand in his. "It's a pleasure to meet you." His hand was soft, but still masculine. When he pulled away, I remember feeling slightly confused by the experience.

Michael was the same age as me, but that first encounter, among others, made him seem much more refined than any guy in their early twenties. If we had met in a bar, I would have pegged him for at least twenty-seven. He carried himself in a way that suggested confidence and pride, but I still found him warm and approachable. He was clearly well known at NYU. Most of the girls in the cohort noticed him for more than his good grades; their eyes following his every move whenever he made his way into class.

As I made my way to my seat, I could have sworn I saw one girl actually slowly scan him with her eyes as he reached over to a retrieve a pen he had dropped on the floor. I caught eyes with her and she quickly turned away, but not before giving me a nasty side-look first.

I laughed to myself and claimed the empty seat next to Michael.

"What's so funny?" he raised an eyebrow.

"Nothing worth mentioning," I smirked.

I pulled out a large notebook from my over-sized purse, and realized I didn't have any pens on me. They must have fallen out while I was dashing through the rain like a crazy person. I rummaged through my bag for another minute until Michael presented me with a pen.

"Thanks," I murmured.

He just nodded and returned his eye to the front of the room. I scanned the lecture hall and quickly noticed our other friends weren't in class today. As if to read my mind, Michael leaned over and said, "Olivia and Alex aren't here. I'm assuming the rain kept them away." He leaned over close enough for me to smell his cologne. He smelled like sandalwood, and something else. As his arm accidentally brushed against mine from leaning a little too close, I quickly pulled it back and smiled. I felt my heart rate pick up a little bit when he touched me, but I shook it off. I had obviously noticed he was a good-looking guy, but I had never thought about him as anything more than just a friend.

Neither Olivia nor Alex lived in Manhattan, so it made sense that they would use the bad weather as an excuse to ditch. I looked around, noticing a lot more empty seats than usual. As I scanned the room, I watched one girl stare at Michael while simultaneously chewing her bottom lip. I raised an eyebrow at her, but she was too busy drooling to notice. Apart from the drooler, most of the class had definitely opted out of today's lecture.

I turned to Michael and whispered, "I'm guessing that's a common theme today."

He smiled and said in a near whisper, "I'm glad *you* made it." I felt a small shudder go through me as his voice dropped into a smooth, lower octave.

I smiled back at Michael and caught his eyes. I felt my stomach drop, the way it does when you're on the top of a really high roller coaster. I could feel heat rise from my chest, into my cheeks, undoubtedly making them flush, and wondered if this cold was turning into fever. As I took a deep breath to get my ever-rapidly climbing heart rate until control, I immediately felt a tickle in my throat. Before I knew it, I began uncontrollably coughing again. Perfect, I thought. I put my hand over my mouth to muffle the sound as much as possible. I was petrified Dr. Van der Stein would kick me out for interrupting his lecture on the myth of phrenology. Just as I was about to get up and run into the hallway, Michael tapped my shoulder and without saying a word reached into his pocket, pulled out a handful of cough drops, and placed them on the desk in front of me. We made eye contact but I couldn't speak to thank him, fearing any use of my voice would trigger another coughing fit. He turned back to face the front of the class but I continued to stare at him. I then stared at the cough drops.

Why was this affecting me so much? I felt a strong sense of panic come over me, followed by a moment of clarity.

I was in love with Michael.

Chapter 2

Tell me you love me

The next day my apartment buzzer went off at exactly 8p.m. Without asking who wanted in, I buzzed back, opening the downstairs entrance, unlocked my door, and plopped back onto my couch. My best friend Cassandra had made me re-tell every moment of yesterday's class with Michael ad nauseum over the phone that afternoon. By the end of it, I chalked up my new-found love for him as nothing more than fever-induced delirium. Even if I had found Michael momentarily attractive, I was looking forward to a nice relaxing evening on the couch with Nicholas. I finished the conversation with Cassandra by telling her that Nicholas was coming over that evening because he wanted to "nurse me back to health".

Cassandra let out a long sigh into the receiver, and almost threateningly said, "We'll talk about this tomorrow."

Two minutes after the buzzer had rung, my door opened and Nicholas Anderson had materialized. He was just standing there, smiling warmly at me. He was wearing his traditional torn jeans, plain white sneakers, and a dark-blue T-shirt with a hoodie over it. He topped the look off with a worn-out gray baseball-style hat that I remember him buying four years ago at Abercrombie. Nicholas was always a jeans and T-shirt kind of guy, he never dressed to impress anyone, always appearing completely comfortable, and he effectively pulled it off. It was one of the things that had drawn me to him in the first place.

We had met four years ago, freshman year of college at Rutgers when my roommate Dasha had introduced us. We clicked instantly and became fast friends, bonding over our mutual hatred of our economics professor and our love for Dashboard Confessional's music. Even though the economics class would be the only class we would take together, me being a combined Biological Sciences/ Psychology major, and him being a Communications major, we still made it a point to spend nearly every day together. At this time, four years ago, I was still involved with my high-school sweetheart and didn't think of Nicholas as more than just a good buddy. By the time we finished undergrad, I came to think of him as one of my best friends. It wasn't until one rainy Friday night two years ago when Nicholas insisted on coming over to talk and said that it was extremely important. He refused to tell me any details over the phone, which only made me imagine the worst. I was so nervous from his evasiveness, figuring something horrible had happened, that I immediately grabbed and hugged him when he arrived that evening. I nervously looked him up and down for some sort of clue as to what was going on. He quickly realized my frantic state and let out a chuckle.

"It's nothing bad, Amalia," he said, leading me to the couch. "I'm sorry I scared you. I just had to talk to you in person, and it had to be *now*."

Dying of anticipation, I put my hands on his shoulders and commanded, "Tell me now."

He took my hands off his shoulders and held on to them tightly, all the while keeping strong eye contact. Taken aback by this gesture, I was beginning to feel nervous. He let go of my left hand and stroked my out-grown bangs away from my face.

Without breaking eye contact, he said "I know we've been friends for a long time." Nicholas paused and finally broke eye

15

contact. He sheepishly looked down at the floor, almost too embarrassed or afraid to continue with his obviously well-prepared speech.

I opened my mouth to break the silence when he said, "But I'm crazy about you, and I have been since the first time I saw you."

My initial reaction was to bypass this type of emotionally charged contact with a joke, but I was too stunned to deflect with my usual sarcasm. Nicholas then proceeded to proverbially pour his heart out to me, recapping every moment of the first day we met, from the smell of the perfume I had on, right down to the green laces in my sneakers, and everything in between. He ended his pontification perfectly, declaring the words that every girl longs to hear from a man.

He cupped my face in his hands and softly said, "Amalia, you're the one".

I was petrified. No one had ever told me I was "the one", and certainly never with such conviction and confidence that Nicholas had presented. He spoke as if the alternative, me not being "the one", was impossible. After taking a few days to think about this proposal, of him and I taking a huge leap into a full-blown relationship that could end badly, ultimately causing us to never speak again, I decided it was worth the risk if it meant I got to be with someone who loved me so intensely. It was now two years later, and I had never felt happier.

Remembering that night only made me feel more relieved and comforted by his familiar presence when he walked over to me tonight.

"I come bearing gifts!" he said as he excitedly reached into a plastic Duane Reade bag.

I wrapped the blanket around me and sank a little lower into the couch, fully preparing myself to be taken care of. Even with his cap on, I could see that Nicholas's dark hair had grown out well past the point of needing a haircut, but somehow it only made him look sexier.

"Nyquil, tissues, organic green tea, and Vitamin C," he proudly presented as he systematically placed the contents of the bag in a line on my coffee table.

After emptying the contents of the bag, he took off his hat and threw it on the table, revealing his perfectly straight, gorgeous jet-black hair. He then leaned over me and put his hand on my forehead; his hands were always warm and comforting. I immediately closed my eyes in reaction to the warm rush of what I could only recognize as love. True love that formed when you knew someone perfectly for years before you even began dating them, not the kind of quick lust that was elicited when a near-stranger offers you a lozenge. Having been raised by an atheist mother, the notion of faith to me was as well received as believing in the tooth fairy. However, when it came to Nicholas, the cynical, black-and-white realist that had been ingrained in me from an early age seemed to disappear. I firmly believed that we were meant to be soul-mates. I opened my eyes and stared into his. His eyes were by far his best feature. They were perfectly round and impossibly wide and youthful, a light chestnut color with flakes of deep brown, which masculinized an otherwise feminine trait.

"Hi, baby," I purred dreamily, slipping further into bliss. His strong arms were exactly what I needed to fall into after a day of feeling awful.

"Hello, darling," he answered sweetly, stroking my hair and pulling me closer to him.

I could smell his Acqua di Gio cologne, and I was convinced it was the greatest scent in nature. I could feel him breathing as he gently put my heavy head on his chest. All of the chaos and stress of the previous day had vanished. This was exactly what I needed. I felt the warm envelopment of sleep coming.

"Tell me you love me," he whispered as he pushed my hair off of my face.

I smiled, closed my eyes, and took a deep breath. Before I could even take a swig of Nyquil, I was out.

Chapter 3

Dirty Blondes

"You're a damn idiot," Cassie rolled her eyes as she tried to flag down the bartender at Oliver's Tavern.

Except her nasty comment wasn't directly at the cute, hipster bartender, it was directed at me.

"You've been in love with Michael since the first day you met him, I remember you going on and on about how he made you shake his hand," she said, annoyed at both me and now the hipster.

Cassandra was not used to not getting her way, or in this case, her order taken. She was growing increasingly annoyed at the bartender for not paying attention to her despite her best efforts.

I looked around the bar. I couldn't help but notice the place was overly crowded for a Thursday evening, containing mostly an older scene. I checked my watch; it wasn't even nine, way too early for this kind of crowd. Even through all of the yuppie noise, I could hear Third Eye Blind's "Semi-Charmed Life" playing over the speakers and had a brief flashback to summer camp. In the left corner of the room I noticed a group of four good-looking men in suits, probably bankers, laughing too loudly. Finally, the exasperated bartender appeared in front of us.

Before he could even ask what we wanted, Cassandra said, "It's about time! Gin and tonic, and not any of that cheap well shit.

Make sure you put Tanqueray in there." she commanded without even looking up, "I can tell the difference."

A little embarrassed by her tenacity I said sheepishly, "Jack and Coke. Please." Adding the please as an attempt to soften the experience and minimize the chances of spit being in her drink in addition to her high-class gin.

He made the drinks in record time and slammed them down in front of us, spilling a good amount of mine onto the bar, but thankfully missing any of my clothes.

"I mean," she started in again as she plucked the lime out of her drink and dropped it onto the bar, "I can't believe you haven't done anything about this sooner."

She sipped her drink and then finally met my gaze. I suddenly felt very alert.

"Woah, wait a minute, I'm not *doing* anything. What are you talking about?" I said, a little confused by her vigilant attitude.

She looked at me, straw in mouth, and cocked her head to the side as if to say *"You know what I mean."*

"Cass, Michael and I are just friends." I said calmly, hoping to disarm the attack that I knew was coming. Clearly not buying it, Cassandra let out a laugh, but it sounded more like a snort. "Sure, he's a good-looking guy, but I'm not doing anything! For starters, I have a boyfriend who I love." I pressed my hands to my chest, watching as she shook her head at me.

Even though Cassandra was my best friend, she had only met Nicholas a handful of times and for some reason unbeknownst to me, she wasn't his biggest fan. I believed her disdain for him had something to do with the first time they met. He had made a joke about her name; I couldn't recall the details since I was already three or four drinks in when the misunderstanding happened, but the whole ordeal had left a bad taste in Cassie's mouth.

"Secondly," I said and then paused to take a sip of my drink. I suddenly felt a strong relief from the alcohol that was in front of me, "Michael has a girlfriend, in case you had forgotten."

"Hello! Who lives in Phoenix!" she practically shouted, at the same time as the bartender walked by. He shot us a look, and then smiled politely.

"That bartender's pretty cute; you shouldn't be such a bitch to him," I muttered.

"Don't try to change the subject, Amy!" she said, now grinning. She held up one finger and shook her head. Her blonde hair bounced from side to side.

She was the only person on earth who could get away with calling me Amy. After all, Amy is in no way short for Amalia, but in eighth-grade gym class she decided my actual name was too much of a mouthful and has been calling me Amy ever since. She could obviously tell I was not amused by this conversation, so she finally pulled back.

"Fine," she said, softening. "I am sorry I even so much as implied that you could do better than Nicholas Anderson." She crossed her legs and started looking around the bar, as if this conversation was suddenly boring her.

I shook my head and clapped in front of her face to regain her attention. "It's not a question of doing better, Cass. I love Nick, he's my boyfriend. Michael is in a relationship and regardless of geography he and Marge seem to be doing fine, so moving on!" I said in a self-declaring rant, and then downed the rest of my drink.

Cassandra, not knowing when to leave well enough alone concluded with, "Marge, ugh! I even hate her name."

"We're moving on!"

Now I was the one practically yelling.

We both looked at each other and burst out laughing. We've been friends for ten years and had never gotten into a real fight. Sure there were moments when we would get short with each other, but it always ended with a laugh, knowing how ridiculous we sounded. She flipped her short, golden hair back, and gave me a light punch on the shoulder.

"Excuse me," someone said from behind us.

I turned around to a very well-dressed man in what I assumed was an expensive, and well-tailored, suit. It was one of the laughing bankers from the corner. I noticed he had grayish eyes and recalled earlier that day in class, when I had learned how rare that physical trait was. All in all, a good-looking man.

"Are you sisters?" he asked as he leaned in a little closer to us.

When he came closer I could tell he was older than Cassie and I, definitely late twenties or possibly even thirty. I turned to Cassandra, expecting her to answer with some quick retort, but she just sat there, staring at the guy. I felt the need to jump in.

"No, sorry. We're not sisters," I offered, not really sure why I felt the need to apologize, but he seemed completely disinterested in what I had to say and continued looking at Cassandra.

She finally recovered from her swoon and said, "That's right, we're not sisters. People always ask us if we're related, though, because we have the same hair color."

I loosely grabbed a handful of Cassandra's, barely shoulder-length, hair and held it up to my own in an attempt to justify this comment. My hair was about five inches longer than her hair, hanging down the middle of my back. Despite this difference, the coloring was virtually the same.

"Dirty blondes?" he smirked.

I couldn't help but roll my eyes at him. Anyone over the age of 18 should never make a joke that pedestrian. He barely noticed my dismay.

"Bryce Peterson," he said. I work for Ernst and Young, in accounting".

Bryce took a sip of his beer and then continued, "I just started working there this week, so a few of my buddies and I are out celebrating. What are your names? What do you do?"

I thought it was odd that he offered up his credentials without us even asking. Also, his questions were directed at both of us, but it seemed clear he was only interested in Cassandra's answer. I felt relieved; I had enough problems with men right now. For example, I couldn't get the thought of Michael's soft graze against my arm out of my mind. Something so insignificant was suddenly the main focus of most of my thoughts. I couldn't tell Cassandra, she'd never let me hear the end of it. Besides, I felt guilty for ever feeling this way.

"Hello there, Bryce. My name is Cassandra de Luca and I work for Prestige magazine," she said proudly, although it was clear he had never heard of the publication.

Cassandra had just been promoted from intern to publications assistant. I still wasn't entirely sure what her job entailed. "Um hi, I'm Amalia Hastings," I uttered, giving a little wave to Cassandra and Bryce, who appeared to be in a staring contest at this point.

"I'm studying Biology and Behavioral Sciences at NYU; decided to go for my Master's," I continued, but it was no use, the attention was clearly not on me.

I checked my watch again, nine-thirty. If I left now, I might actually be able to get a good night's sleep. I decided to let Cassandra and Bryce talk and call it a night.

"Okay Cassie, have a good night," I called to her and grabbed my purse. "Nice meeting you, Bryce."

"Yeah, sure. Goodnight," she mumbled, seemingly mesmerized by her new crush.

I laughed to myself and then made my way to the door. The cool, crisp fall air felt great when I got outside. It was refreshing after coming out of the stuffy, crowded bar. I smiled and thought about how lucky I was to be living in this city. I started to make my way down Barrow Street when I heard something. It sounded like a twig snapping. The type of sound you hear in a horror movie just before the damsel in distress gets stabbed.

"Amalia?" a voice called. My heart started pounding faster, and this time I couldn't blame it on illness.

"Yes?" I called out. The figure came closer to me and was now in focus. He stood there, smiling and I felt a little dizzy. I took a deep breath and finally spoke, "Hi, Michael."

Chapter 4

I'm all yours

"Thank God you cooked!" I clapped as I walked into Nicholas's studio apartment.

His place was dimly lit, all of the lights were off except for the overhead light in the kitchen.

"Oh, were you hungry? I think I may have some leftovers in the fridge," Nicholas replied jokingly, wryly smiling.

I dropped my purse onto the bed and kicked off my new ballet flats I had just picked up at Necessary Clothing. My bare feet hit the cold hardwood floor, but it felt good after the nine-block walk. I walked over to Nicholas and kissed him hello.

"Ha! You are hilarious," I smiled. "Thanks for agreeing to eat dinner at five like a senior citizen. I wanted to make sure I got to see you today and my class is going to end late tonight."

"Honey, of course! Besides if I didn't cook for you, you'd most likely die of malnutrition. After all, one cannot survive on pasta and whiskey alone. Why do most of your classes start so late anyway?" he asked for what felt like the hundredth time.

I was waiting for him to become irritated with my always having to run off to class or to the library, but he never did. Nick was the perfect boyfriend; patient, understanding, and insanely cute. I watched him cooking for me and I think I fell a little more in

25

love with him.

"Um, I assume it's because most people work until about five or so; so they schedule most graduate level classes at six-thirty or seven," I replied, stroking his hair.

I motioned to him for a hug and placed my head on his chest; my head fit perfectly under his chin, making me feel safe.

"And I don't only survive on pasta and whiskey," I insisted. "There's also scotch and dark chocolate to consider."

He gave me a wink and a quick kiss on the forehead. I crossed over to the fridge and grabbed myself a bottle of water, suddenly feeling warm.

"So, how did last night go?" he asked, catching me off guard.

"It went fine." I answered quickly. "Cassandra met a guy named Bryce something and I started to feel like a third wheel, so I just headed home early."

I felt guilty for lying and couldn't look at him as I answered. I turned to walk out of the kitchen when he grabbed my arm and passionately pulled me towards him, my face less than an inch from his.

"You're burning," I whispered, before he could kiss me.

"What?" he asked, genuinely confused.

I sheepishly replied, "The chicken, it's burning."

I bit my bottom lip and looked up at Nick. After all of this time I was still intensely attracted to him. Whenever I caught a glimpse of those big, gorgeous eyes, I could feel myself melt a little.

Nicholas twisted the knob on the stove, turning off the flame. I let out a small laugh and realized I probably wasn't going to be eating dinner tonight. Then without saying another word he lifted me up and carried me onto the bed. Carefully placing me down, he began removing my clothes while kissing me tenderly. His mouth enveloping mine, sending goosebumps down my back. He quickly peeled off his shirt and jeans, and threw them on the floor. He then stopped and began to look me up and down, admiring every inch of my body. I thought about how lucky I was to have a boyfriend who was so into me, and how I never had to be self-conscious around him. He placed his hand under my chin and looked deeply into my eyes. I felt a surreal moment of tranquility and said, "Take me, I'm all yours." He began kissing my neck, and then my stomach, and then came back up to my lips.

"Dinner's getting cold," I said jokingly.

"The microwave works," he said seductively smiling back at me. "We can reheat it."

I never did make it to class that night. Instead, Nicholas and I finally got around to eating dinner after an amazing hour in bed, opened a bottle of Merlot, and then re-watched our favorite movie, *Fear and Loathing in Las Vegas,* for what had to be the twentieth time. I glanced at the clock; it was a little past midnight. Nick and I had gone to bed about forty minutes ago and he had quickly slipped into a blissful coma-like state. I on the other hand, was wide awake. I felt an overabundance of guilt as I looked over at Nick, because for the past half hour all I could think about was Michael. More specifically, the run-in he and I had last night as I was leaving Oliver's Tavern. I turned on my back and replayed last night's scene in my mind.

"Heading home?" Michael had asked. As soon as he spoke I felt a shiver of excitement rush through my body.

"Yeah. I'm beat," I answered, trying to sound as casual as possible.

I felt the need to keep the conversation going, but a cold gust of air hit my face and made it impossible to think of something charming to say. I glanced down the street behind Michael and I noticed a young couple walking by. Their arms were linked as they made their way into a subway entrance. I wondered if they were in a relationship, or merely a second date.

"So, um. What are you doing in this neighborhood, alone?"

I knew Michael lived in midtown, East 60th street; not exactly close by.

"I just left a friend's apartment, they live nearby. I needed to walk for a bit and clear my head."

I felt a sense of worry and intrigue, as if he wasn't telling me something important, his usual composed and refined disposition seemed a little shaky.

"Are you alright? I mean, do you want some company?" I asked as I reached out to touch his arm.

"I was just going to head back to my apartment, why don't you come over for a drink and you can tell me what's bothering you?"

Shit! What was I doing inviting him back to my apartment, at night? I couldn't stop myself, though; it was as if my mind had no control over my speech. I was suddenly eager to help Michael in any way I could, and apparently that meant inviting him back to my apartment.

"I—" he started. Then he paused for a minute, and I silently braced myself for rejection. "Amalia, I would love to come in for a drink. I could really use someone to talk to."

"Great!" I said, a little too eagerly. "I mean, that's cool. Let's get going." I tried to sound more composed, motioning toward the crosswalk.

He smiled and moved a bit closer to me. I immediately went weak at the knees. In all of my anxiety, I hadn't noticed how great he looked until right now. Michael always dressed well but for some reason I took extra notice of his fitted black button-down shirt, dark denim jeans free of distress of any kind, and loafers to pull the look together. I realized I was still staring at him when he pulled me in for a hug.

"Thank you, Amalia. You're a great friend," he whispered.

I felt strong sense of disappointment and a little foolish as he let go of me. A friend? A buddy? Is that all Michael thought of me as? More importantly, why did I care so much?

Chapter 5

Olivia

"Oh my gosh how many times do I have to say this to you? Nothing happened!" I said for what had to be the third time in five minutes. Olivia and I had decided to grab a drink at Fat Black Pussy Cat after class that evening, and Cassandra insisted on coming along. Michael and Alex also jumped on the idea to drink away Dr. Van der Stein's lecture on organic chemistry, and were meeting us soon. "*Non capisco!* I just don't understand you!" Cassandra threw her arms up and shook her head at me, her chandelier earrings bouncing from side to side.

"Woah, was that English?" Olivia said with a huge smile on her face, obviously entertained by Cassandra's latest outburst.

"Please don't encourage her, Olivia," I buried my face in my hands.

"You have this good-looking guy, alone in your apartment," Cassandra continued to berate me, ignoring Olivia's question. But before she could finish, I interrupted.

I held up my right hand. "Christina was home, we were not alone," I said declaratively, as if that was some sort of justification for my lie.

"Oh really? Was she in the living room with the two of you? Or was she once again cooped up in her bedroom reading some obscure novel and being completely antisocial?" Cassandra cocked her head to the side and raised an eyebrow.

"Jeeze!" I shook my head." First you attack me, now Christina?"

Olivia just sat there in silent bewilderment, her light-brown eyes as wide as possible. She had met Cassie several times before but was still confused by her boisterous demeanor. Olivia was the polar opposite of Cassandra and I. Being that we were both from Staten Island, Cassie and I prided ourselves on being loud, outspoken, and at times bitchy. Olivia on the other hand was from Providence, Rhode Island. Having only moved to New York four months ago, she was still quiet, polite, very shy, and free of any New York City-style dialect. She had attended college at the University of Florida. No city experience what-so-ever. Olivia had "newcomer writer" all over her. The only unpolished thing she did was smoke Newports. I found it to be very uncharacteristic of her, but it did give her a little bit of an edge. However, despite their differences, the two got along famously, as if they balanced each other out.

"*Dire*! Just answer the question!" Cassie demanded, her hazel eyes flashing.

Being that her grandparents were right off the boat from Italy, they demanded she learn to speak Italian and this she bestowed upon us when she was excited.

"Were you, or were you not, alone with him?"

I felt defeated.

"I was, alright, but nothing happened!" I said for now the fifth time. "Also, can we stick to English tonight?"

Cassandra smiled triumphantly.

Through all of my annoyance, I felt a smile tug at the sides of my lips.

"I'm going to slap you," I said jokingly.

Olivia shook her head at the two of us, a wide grin decorating her face.

"I'm going to record the two of you and upload it when you

31

aren't looking," she said laughing at us.

She reached into her gorgeous Michael Kors purse and pulled out her cell.

"Oh hey guys, it's actually almost nine thirty. Michael and Alex are going to be here any minute, so maybe it would be a good idea to cap this conversation until tomorrow?" she asked.

"You know what?" I leaned forward. "No need to, ladies, because I am done pretending. Cassandra, you were right all along. We did it, Michael and me. We had hot, dirty sex right on my Ikea couch all while Christina was in the next room. It was amazing. I mean, it was the kind of sex you could only have when you've been stuck screwing the same person for years, boy did I let go of my inhibitions. Phew! Feels so good to get that off my chest!" I slammed my right hand down on the table, hoping this would finally shut Cassie up.

Olivia burst out laughing and then raised her glass of wine to toast me. Thinking I had finally silenced her, I shot Cassandra a look.

Cassandra gave me a blank, unamused stare, and flipped her hair back. "Fine, but Amalia, this conversation is not over. I'm heading to the ladies."

She dramatically pushed her chair in and marched to the ladies' room.

"C'mon! Champagne for everyone! Don't you want to know if he wears boxers or briefs?" I shouted to her as she walked away.

Her three-inch heels clacked loudly on the bar's old wooden floors. Every man at the bar turned to watch Cassie walk. Having come straight from her office, she was wearing dark-gray dress pants, patent-leather pumps, a bright-red button-down top, and oversized chandelier earrings. I had to hand it to the girl, she looked great. Suddenly feeling self-conscious about my own outfit, a dark-brown dress paired with gray blazer and a jeweled head-band, I turned to Olivia. She was wearing a lime-green cardigan with a white camisole underneath, a knee-length black pleated skirt, and understated basic black flats. Her mousy brown hair was pulled back into a plain pony tail, minimal jewelry, and from what I could tell no make-up other than clear lip gloss. I couldn't help but wonder if she felt underdressed. Before I could complete the thought, I suddenly felt two hands on my shoulder, causing me to nearly jump out of my seat. I quickly turned around to see who it was.

"I always say it, Hastings, you're too highly strung," Alex said, holding on to me tightly.

"Maybe it's because of the lack of personal space I have in this bar," I countered, as he continued to hold onto my shoulders.

I brushed him off, and wondered why Michael was friends with him. He and Michael had appeared out of nowhere wearing what appeared to be matching outfits. They both had on dark denim jeans, loafers, and button-down shirts with fitted v-neck sweaters over them, allowing the pattern of the shirt collar and cuffs to show. I pretended to be disgusted and dust off my shoulders.

"Hey you two," said Michael, pulling an empty bar stool from a neighboring table.

"So how ridiculous was Dr. Van Der's class today?"

"Oh no!" Cassandra said as she strutted back to her seat. "If you're going to talk about class, I'm out of here!"

Cassandra was the only one at the table who did not currently take classes at NYU.

"Who are you?" she said to Alex.

"Hey, I'm Alex", he said, holding his hand out, seemingly unfazed by her sharp question. "You must be Cassandra."

"Another hand-shaker, eh?" she said sarcastically.

I kicked her under the table and shot her a look of warning. Her iPhone started to vibrate, shaking the entire table.

"It's Bryce," she explained.

A smile crept across her face, and something made me think it was a booty call.

"The yuppie from Oliver's?" I grimaced; a little disappointed she was seeing him again.

"That's the one," she answered without looking up from her phone. "I forgot I was supposed to be meeting him. I have to run. Boys, always a pleasure. *Arrivederci.*"

"Goodnight," we all said in unison.

"Who's Bryce again?" asked Olivia.

"Ugh, you don't want to know," I shook my head.

The bar was starting to clear out, thankfully. In New York City, no one was ever home. Most of the population inhabited bars or boutique coffee shops instead of ever returning to their respective homes. I couldn't decide if it was the size of their apartments that kept them away, or the constant need to feel "busy."

I caught Michael's eye and for a second I forgot anyone else was with us. He smiled at me and the increasingly familiar rush of heat started to creep up on me.

"So, Amalia," Alex said, breaking me out of my daze. "I heard you're going to Panama when school's over in the spring."

"Brazil," I answered quickly.

"Same shit," he shot back.

"Actually, they're two completely separate countries," I answered, annoyed at his ignorance and attitude.

Alex and I had always had a love-hate relationship, and he was closer with Michael and Olivia than me, but I tolerated him for the sense of the group.

"Whatever, they speak Spanish there don't they?" he smiled sarcastically.

"No. Actually, they speak Portuguese. Seriously dude, get a map," I mumbled and took a sip of my beer.

"Brazil! That's so exciting!" Olivia said, trying to recover the uncomfortable moment.

Michael looked up at me and said, "I didn't know you were leaving the country! For how long?"

"About three months", I answered. "I'll be there from the end of May until August. I have a cousin who lives there so I am going to spend some time living with the locals."

"Are you going for your job?" he asked.

"No, nothing like that," I shrugged. "I've just always wanted to go there; it just looks so beautiful. I spent all of last summer working as a receptionist so I could save enough money to buy a plane ticket."

"Very ambitious, Amalia. What does your boyfriend have to say about that?" Alex asked, challenging me.

"Nothing. He feels fine," I shot back.

No need to go into details, to explain Nicholas and I had gotten into a small argument that morning over the length of time I was going to be away. Our minor argument was none of Alex's business, and also I didn't want Michael to think Nick and I had any problems at all.

"Well, I could use a smoke," Olivia said to Alex, attempting to break the tension. "Care to join me?" She could tell I was getting annoyed by him and gave me a small smile. He nodded and stood up, motioning for her to walk in front of him. As obnoxious as he was, he had good manners. I was relieved to have the questions stop, and also to be alone with Michael. I noticed once again how well put together he looked and wondered how he looked when at home, alone, with no one to impress.

"Hey, listen sorry I skipped out last night with just a note," he leaned closer over the table.

His cologne smelled very masculine, like deep sandalwood and a touch of something else I couldn't quite put my finger on. He leaned back in his chair and laughed. "It's just that, you looked so peaceful, I didn't want to wake you."

"Yeah, um, don't worry about it," I muttered nervously. I tucked a stray curl behind my ear and sat up a little straighter. "I'm just embarrassed I fell asleep!"

I was definitely more disappointed than embarrassed, having wasted my time with him unconscious. After I ran into him on the street two nights ago, Michael had come back to my apartment to talk. After opening a bottle of Pinot and pouring us both two oversized glasses, I asked him what was bothering him.

"I'd actually rather not discuss it," he said. "Is it alright if we just sit here?"

I wasn't quite sure what to say. Our reason for being at my place alone was gone, and I felt even more awkward than before.

"Yeah, sure," I replied, noticeably confused by the request. "Anything to help."

The night was, as I told the girls, uneventful. After we finished the wine, we sat and talked about school, applying for internships, and what our lives were like before we moved to New York. Apparently I had been so exhausted that I fell asleep on the couch while we were watching *The Daily Show*.

I woke up the next morning, still on the couch, with a throw blanket around me and a note on the coffee table that read, "*Thanks for the company, see you in class.*"

My assumption was right, that Michael had left right after I fell asleep. I looked around and noticed the bar was emptying out. Now this was more like it, no fighting over the bartenders tonight.

"So, um, how's Marge doing?" I asked, and then immediately regretted the words.

He seemed a little taken back by the question. The only information I had on Michael's girlfriend was her name, and the fact that she was two years younger. Since she was still in college, a senior at Arizona State, they only saw each other once every month or two.

"She's doing fine. I spoke to her earlier today on the phone, but it's not the same," he said. "Long-distance relationships are hard. Even harder when you're older. I mean, I'm not an undergrad any more."

I looked at him surprised. I wasn't expecting such a detailed answer.

"Anyway, isn't your birthday coming up? Twenty-three right? Getting old," he said playfully, obviously changing the subject.

I played along.

"Yeah, next week," I mumbled. "Don't remind me."

"Ha, not a birthday person?" he asked, looking amused, and gave me a poke on the shoulder.

"No, actually I'm not. Does it matter?" I answered, now laughing myself. "You're all going to make me do something lame anyway!"

"No way! We're going to have fun," he motioned to the bartender.

I cocked my head to the side and said, "Michael, every time you say we're going to have fun, we end up drunk, completely broke, and lost in neighborhoods *no one* should ever be lost in."

"Yes, Amalia," he smiled at me, flashing every one of his perfectly straight teeth. "That is how I define fun."

Chapter 6

It's my birthday, and I'll do what I want to

I looked around Cassandra's spacious two-bedroom apartment crowded with about twenty of my closest friends. The place was filled with pink and white balloons, plastic martini glasses, and paper decorations including a custom banner that read "Happy Birthday Amalia!"

I thought back to when she and Nicholas had asked me what I wanted to do for my birthday when we were hanging out last week.

"Just a dinner with the two of you, Olivia, and Christina," I replied. "Nothing too fancy, maybe Max Brenner? Or even somewhere in Little Italy would be perfect. You know, something simple."

My input, however, had been clearly ignored. Lured to Cassie's place under the false pretenses of going to said "low key" dinner, I nearly had a heart attack when the energetic guests of my clandestinely planned surprise party jumped out at me.

"Surprise!" everyone yelled in unison.

"What the hell! The two of you are in so much trouble!" I said as I caught my breath. I leaned over the couch, pretending they had given me a heart attack.

"Were you surprised, honey?" Nicholas asked with a sinister

smirk on his face.

"Yeah, I mean I thought we were having a small, intimate dinner?"

He leaned in for a kiss and I turned away, playfully pretending to be too annoyed for affection. A few seconds later, I was bombarded with drink offers and birthday wishes.

"Happy Birthday, Hastings," said Alex as he handed me a glass of champagne.

"Twenty-three!" Olivia enthusiastically threw her arms around me. "It's about time!"

Since my birthday was at the beginning of October, I was the last of my friends to have a birthday this year. I had been teased by friends for being the youngest essentially my whole life.

"The food is delicious, by the way. I got that vegetarian place Blossom to cater. Great turn-out too; everyone is here," Olivia said, smiling brightly.

Her eyes were wide and covered in gray glitter eye-shadow.

"I could use some of that food," I muttered, scanning the room for sustenance.

"Right this way!" she said, leading me by the hand.

I numbly followed Olivia as she led me through Cassandra's apartment. I swallowed hard and smiled, trying my best to hide the anxiety that this surprise birthday party was causing me. On the way to the kitchen, I quickly scanned the room to see if indeed *everyone* was here. I saw my one roommate, Christina, in the corner talking to some girl I had never met. Cassandra was on the living room couch kissing her new boyfriend, Bryce. Alex, check. Olivia, check. Nicholas, check. I even recognized a few people from class Olivia must have told Cassandra to invite. Everyone was in fact accounted for; everyone other than Michael.

I swallowed my champagne and grabbed another. I might as well make the best of this situation.

As the night went on, my friends became progressively drunk, which unfortunately included Nicholas. Out of nowhere, he decided now would be a perfect time to discuss my summer trip to Brazil.

"I just don't understand why you feel the need to leave the country for two months," he said in a tone I had only heard him use once before.

During the first year of our relationship, his mother passed away during a family weekend in college. It was quick and without warning. She was hit by a drunk driver while crossing the street in downtown New Brunswick, where Rutgers was. Neither of us saw this, but I'll never forget the acidic taste that filled my mouth that Tuesday afternoon when Nick got a call from Robert Wood Johnson hospital. By the time we got there, it was too late to say our goodbyes. His mom died in the ambulance during transport. For the next few months, Nick was cold to me. The more I tried to support and be there for him, the more he'd pull away. I found myself chasing after what we'd had, desperately clinging to those first nine months together when he thought I was perfect. It took about six more months of me putting up with his callous demeanor until he finally started to come around and act like the guy I knew and loved. He apologized for the way he'd treated me, and I forgave him instantly. I didn't know what it was like to lose a parent, and couldn't have understood what he was going through.

But now, as I stood here in Cassandra's apartment I felt sick, like I had eaten something bad. My eyes filled up with tears and I quickly turned my face away from the crowd. If Nick was capable of acting the way he did when his mother died, it's possible that darkness was something that was inside of him, and could crawl out at any moment.

He dragged me into Cassandra's bedroom, saying we needed to talk more. I felt my heart sink into my stomach, and found myself wishing I hadn't drank that second glass of champagne. I closed the door to Cassandra's bedroom and immediately began speaking.

"Baby, it's not that long," I pleaded with him.

I shook my head and gave him a weary smile. Anxious to end this argument, I softly took his hands in mine and looked right into his eyes.

"Besides, you'll be starting an internship around the time I leave," I said, trying to ease the blow. "You'll be so busy by the time summer comes along, we'd barely have time to see each other in the first place. That's why I picked those two months to be there."

It was true, Nicholas had applied for an internship at Clear Channel in an attempt to find a new job. He would be interning three days a week, without pay, on top of his current workload at his present job. I thought it would be a perfect time for him to get his life together. Just as I thought I was getting through to him, he shook his head, jerked his hands out of my grasp, and started to pace across the room.

"I just expected you to be there for me while I was starting a new position. I'm going to be extremely stressed with all of the new responsibility and it would be nice to be able to come home to my girlfriend, who should be taking care of me," he was practically shouting now. "Not running off to fulfill some ridiculous fantasy to travel the world."

I stood there, stunned. Nicholas had a few drinks in him but I couldn't imagine the alcohol could provoke such a hateful and selfish statement. His eyes, which were normally wide and welcoming, were narrowed. I searched for the words to address this situation calmly.

"Where is this coming from? You've known about this trip for a while now. Nicholas, I think you should take a step back and listen to what you are saying to me. I am not running off to fulfill any sort of fantasy. What you're saying to me is a little selfish."

I walked over to him and gave him a hug. He stood there still, arms defiantly pressed against his own body.

"Now why don't we just go back outside and join the rest of the party; people are probably wondering where I am. We can talk about this tomorrow, I promise."

"All right, Amalia, whatever you want," he uttered dryly. Nicholas never called me by my name. The formality of it made him seem cold and detached, like a scolding grammar-school teacher. It made me a little nervous.

"So will you come back to the party with me, then?" I asked, hopeful we could still salvage the evening.

Without answering me, Nicholas walked out of the bedroom and made a beeline for the living room.

"Where are you going?" I asked.

He grabbed his jacket off the couch and turned to me and said, "I'm going home. Have a wonderful evening."

Before I could open my mouth to answer, he had slammed the door and left. Thankfully the music and chatter was too loud for anyone to have witnessed his temper tantrum. Feeling like I could hardly stand, I sat down on the couch, stunned by the events that had just transpired. This was officially the worst birthday in a very long time. I tried to cry, but nothing came.

After a few minutes of sitting and staring at Cassandra's deep-brown, hardwood floor, I walked back into Cassandra's bedroom and retrieved my cell phone from my purse. In much need of cheering up, I was hoping for a message from Michael, but there was nothing. Fueled by my accelerating anger and two glasses of cheap champagne, I scrolled down my address book, found his name, and hit dial. I felt the need to know, no, demand, where he was and what was so important he couldn't at the very least stop by for an hour or two. After all, the rule usually is that on your birthday, you can do whatever you want. You can drink until you vomit, you can have sex with a stranger, hell you can put on a wig and call yourself by a different name if you so fancy, so what was wrong with a harmless phone call?

The phone rang three times before I heard, "You've reached the voicemail of Michael Rathbourne. Leave a message at the—"

I didn't even let the pre-recorded version of him finish before throwing my phone down onto Cassandra's bed and starting to tear up. I sat on the bed for a few minutes longer and wondering if anyone would notice I was gone, and would come looking for me. No one did. Five minutes later, still sitting on Cassandra's bed, I felt my phone vibrating. A text message from Michael. Finally, I thought, he's probably on his way.

I opened the message. "Sorry I couldn't make it, have a drink for me!"

I read the message again, sure that I was mistaken. That's it? He didn't even wish me Happy Birthday. The tears were starting to fall harder and I decided it was time to go home. I crept out of Cassandra's bedroom, grabbed an unopened bottle of wine from the kitchen, and when no one was looking in my direction, slipped through the front door.

Chapter 7

It's too late honey, and it's too bad

For the three days, Nicholas barely spoke to me. After our fight at my surprise-party-gone-awry, I hadn't been getting much sleep. I couldn't shake the feeling that something was really wrong. The fact was, Nicholas and I never fought, and I didn't know how to handle it. I hadn't seen him since he stormed out of Cassandra's apartment, and our last few phone conversations had been brief and monotonous. His usual "good night" phone call, in which we recapped our entire days to each other, had been replaced with a quick text message, or nothing at all. Although he wasn't blatantly ignoring me, the usual amount of effort he put into grooming our relationship had fallen short. Very short. It wasn't until this afternoon when I was in anatomy class that I finally received a text message from Nick, asking me if I could come over to his apartment afterwards.

When I had gotten to class earlier that day, I had made a concerted effort to ignore Michael, positioning myself on the other side of the auditorium-sized classroom. Sure, I was being juvenile, but I was still hurt from his absence at my party. I used to feel so safe and comfortable with my life.

Thoughts of Nicholas flooded my head, making concentration on the lecture extremely difficult. I glanced at my watch and realized class was almost over. I couldn't wait to see him.

When the professor said, "Until next week, class," I knew I was in the clear to dart out of the classroom.

I quickly headed outside and hailed a cab to Nicholas's apartment. Much to my happiness, a cab pulled up immediately.

"Where to, missy?" the driver said, through a thick accent.

"10th Street and Avenue A!" I spat out.

Since I was in the Washington Square area, I probably could have walked to the Lower East Side, but I was too anxious to see Nicholas and to put this whole fight behind us. A short cab ride later, I was outside Nick's apartment. I feverishly hit the buzzer three times until the door unlocked. I threw open the heavy front door, ran up the four flights of stairs, and burst through his door. Ready to be greeted by a hug and an apology, I was disappointed to see Nicholas sitting on his bed, making no effort to even stand up and give me a proper greeting. Warm beads of sweat rolled down my back as my paranoia accelerated.

Feeling defeated, I slowly closed the door behind me and cautiously made my way over to him, careful not to make any sudden movement.

"Hey," I said, tiptoeing toward him. "Baby, are you okay?"

Upon closer inspection, Nicholas looked upset, as if he had been crying. He was dressed down even more than usual, wearing nothing but a plain white undershirt and baggy gray sweatpants, which he usually reserved for times when he was too sick to dress himself. A wave of horror flooded over me. Something was really wrong.

"Listen," he started.

I braced myself for the bad news.

My mind flooded with a thousand possibilities. Had he gotten fired? Had someone in his family taken ill? Was he being evicted? I sat next to him on the floor and placed my hands on his knees.

"What is it, Nick?" I asked. I folded my hands behind my back, after realizing I had been anxiously peeking at my cuticles for a few minutes.

He still wouldn't look at me. His brown hair hung over his gorgeous eyes, making it impossible for me to feel connected. I cautiously lifted up my right hand and pushed a few strands of hair out of his face.

Without even looking up to meet my gaze he said, "I can't be with you."

The air went out of the room, as though a huge force had hit me in the chest. My head started to spin and I felt more fear than I had ever felt before.

Can't be with me?

I shook my head and squinted. "What do you mean?" I asked, unable to speak louder than a whisper.

Still not looking at me, he unleashed his well-prepared speech.

"I don't know what happened, Amalia, but I just don't feel it anymore."

His words sounded so cold and formal, he couldn't have been talking about us like that, not with such emptiness and detachment. He finally lifted his head up, but still refused to look me in the eyes. Anger momentarily replaced my sadness, and with it came a warm pressure behind my eyes that made its way down to my chest. My head was suddenly killing me and I was having a hard time concentrating. I couldn't recall a time I had ever felt this angry with him. I wanted to tell him what a coward he was being, but I couldn't form the words.

"You were all I ever wanted, for so long. I even remember what you were wearing the first day I met you," he said in a breathy voice. "But I don't feel like that person anymore. I don't feel like that guy you met back in college. And I think, no I know, I need time alone to figure out what I want out of life."

Heavy flows of tears streamed down my face. How could this be happening?

"Whatever this is, we can work through it," I muttered, through sobs.

Finally looking right at me, Nicholas took a deep breath and said, "No. Honey, it's too late."

There was no way I could just give up and accept this.

"Just give it some time, please! I know you're angry with me for going on my trip but we can talk about it. It's not like I am moving to Brazil, this can't just be about me not being there when you start your internship," I pleaded.

"Why are you even going?" he said, this time looking right at me.

"Because I have always wanted to go," I said. "I've always been honest about how much I want to travel. Obviously I can't get up and leave the country whenever I want, but that's why I booked this so far in advance. And honestly, it's something I am doing, for me."

"Well I think that sounds really selfish." he said.

"Please just tell me why you think that's selfish, and we can figure this out together," I pleaded. As I listened to myself speak, I knew I was in the right. I didn't believe what I was doing was selfish at all, but I was willing to put my pride on the back-burner to salvage my relationship.

But it was no use. Nicholas stood up and walked over to the kitchen. He came back to the bed and handed me a box.

"Here, I packed all of your things," he said coldly.

It suddenly dawned on me that this wasn't an impulsive decision. Nicholas must have been planning to break up with me for a few days, if he had taken the time to pack up my things.

"What the hell is this? You've wanted to be with me for so long, for years!" I cried. "You convinced me to be with you, coerced me into falling in love with you, and now after one fight that doesn't even have to really do with our relationship, you're leaving me?"

I was crying, hard. Harder than I had ever cried before. I expected him to listen to me, to consider my words and realize he was being foolish and impulsive. I expected him to grab me and say I was right, that he made a mistake and to forget he had even brought any of this nonsense up, but all he said was, "Yes."

I let out a whimper. As angry as I was, I couldn't express it. My anger felt caged and controlled, by my overwhelming confusion and sadness.

"We belong together, we can fix this. We can fix anything," I uttered with the last drop of fight in me.

But I knew it was useless, that it was over.

"No, Amalia. We can't."

Still sitting on the floor, I watched as he walked over to the front door and held it open for me to leave. I peeled myself off the floor and grabbed the box of my belongings. Without any hope of changing his mind, I looked him in the eyes and said, "I love you, and I will never get over this."

With no emotion or remorse, he looked at the front door and then glanced back at me.

"That's too bad."

Chapter 8

Liz

"Amalia?" someone whispered sweetly. "Wake up, please."

I opened my eyes and found Olivia standing over my bed, holding a mug of what appeared to be coffee in one hand, and a stack of papers in the other.

"Please go away," I mumbled through sobs, pulling the plush covers back over my face.

The cheap, worn-out mattress was the only comfort I had felt in days, and I certainly wasn't going to give it up.

"You have to get up," she said, "You haven't left this apartment in five days and I'm really worried about you."

Besides Olivia's daily check-ins and running into Christina in the kitchen, I hadn't had contact with anyone in almost a week. Christina had continued to buzz Olivia up, most likely relieved she didn't have to deal with my melancholy herself. Every grueling moment spent awake was occupied by an influx of thoughts about Nicholas. I had been crying from the minute I woke up, until the minute I went to sleep every day since he left. I had finally found it easier to just stay asleep than deal with the all-consuming pain.

"Listen," Olivia said, tenderly. "I brought you all of the work you missed during the past few lectures. I also put some hot tea on your nightstand; it's my mother's recipe and it always makes me feel better.

"Thank you," I said, still crying.

Olivia let out a soft sigh. "I have to meet Alex, we are going to study for the exam on Monday. You should really come with us, you've missed a lot of work."

"No," was the only word I could muster up.

"Alright," Olivia said as she rubbed my head through the blanket. "If you need anything at all, call me."

The next thing I knew, it was Monday. I had spent an entire week crying in bed, I felt pathetic and more than a little nauseous. I pushed the comforter off my face, revealing a well-earned pillow crease, and rubbed my stinging eyes.

Through a blur, I looked over at the clock, 9a.m. I couldn't stay in bed today; today I had a midterm. A midterm covering every minute detail of material we had covered in class starting from the first day. A midterm that I had not spent one minute studying for. Not taking a shower for three days really makes you appreciate one, even with my apartment's insufficient water pressure. I walked out of the bathroom and almost collided with not Christina but Liz, my other roommate. Liz and Christina "shared" the master bedroom together, but Christina essentially had the entire room to herself, because since we all moved in at the end of August, Liz had spent exactly three nights sleeping here. She spent most of her time in Queens with her much older boyfriend Tim, who was an aspiring musician. Or maybe he was a painter.

I was grateful she was here today because the shock of her presence distracted me from my pain.

"Amalia, darling, I was hoping to run into you," she said, taking a sip of something from a reusable water bottle.

I found this sentence bizarre, being that we lived together you wouldn't think your roommate would have to hope to "run into you". Liz was wearing a dark-green, floor-length cotton dress, shoes made out of a material that I was sure had to have been previously recycled, with black fishnet stockings and a cropped black motorcycle jacket. She was wearing her bright-red hair pulled back into a tight chignon, and her bright-green eyes were rimmed with silver eyeliner, creating an alluring contrast.

"There's going to be a mixer this weekend, the NYU alumni association is hosting it; as you know I'm on the committee," she said, even though I had no prior knowledge of this. "You are invited, as well as your friends. I expect to see you there."

Before I could open my mouth to decline the offer, she had closed her bedroom door. I made a mental note to start looking for a new roommate for next year. Although, I was thankful for her random appearance, and the "Nicholas-free" five minutes she gave me were like a tropical vacation.

The truth was, this wasn't a feeling that was new to me. I had dated my high-school boyfriend for a year, and when he broke up with me to go away to college a year before I did, I spent the better part of my senior year sulking. I didn't get the support and kind words from my mother that Olivia offered me. She essentially would just walk into my room, see I was still in shambles, and offer me a guttural sound before turning around and walking back out. It seemed like I was always the one getting dumped, never the one doing the dumping.

Time was moving a lot more slowly these past few days, and even after a lengthy shower, I realized I still had about forty minutes before class. Rummaging through my closet, I felt suddenly exhausted by the task of dressing myself. I grabbed the first pair of jeans I saw and threw them on. They were too big, practically falling off. It was the same with two other pairs. Realizing that my lost week unconscious in bed had prevented me from polishing off a few meals, I settled on an old dress that my mother had given me last year for my birthday. I held the dowdy garment up to the mirror and studied it. It was a pale pink, an inappropriate color for the end of November, falling right above the knee (only now it hung a little lower since I had less to hold it up), with a light lace embroidery around the waist. All in all, the dress was hideous. I must have lost myself in a daze because as slow as time moved, I realized I would have to leave in ten minutes if I wanted to make it to this shit show of a midterm on time, so I conceded to the frock. I reached for my chocolate-brown cardigan to put over the dress and slipped on a gray, suede pair of knee-high boots. My hair had already air-dried at this point, so I added a head band to help conceal the frizz. The only thing I was pleased about this morning was the look of my skin. Turns out a week away from soot, wind, and free radicals will do wonders for the complexion. I swept on some blush, one coat of mascara, and added some clear lip gloss. I took a step back to examine myself in the floor-length mirror. I looked like a crazy doll.

I was ripped out of my self-critique by the sound of my phone vibrating. It was a text message from Cassandra. It read, "I hope you're feeling better and you ace your midterm! Also, Christina told me about an affair your other roommate is arranging, sounds like you have fun weekend plans!"

I dropped the phone into my purse and let out a sigh. I was in no condition to go to the mixer this weekend, but it seemed as if I wasn't going to have a choice. I felt a sudden wave of sadness rush over me when I realized this was the first of many upcoming events that I would be attending solo. Trying to push the thought into the back of my head, I grabbed my coat and braced myself for the walk to school.

When I got to class, I was immediately greeted by Olivia.

"You're here!" she practically squealed as she threw her arms around me. "And you're wearing, well, you're wearing something besides your pajamas, so that's a step in the right direction."

She looked my outfit up and down, the whole time keeping a fake smile plastered on her face.

"I was so worried you wouldn't make it and I'd have to come up with some excuse as to why you weren't here. I was going to go with death in the family; I feel like no one ever really checks up on that," she shrugged.

While listening to Olivia's rant, I felt a tap on my shoulder. As if the universe was single-handedly trying to see how much torture I could take, I turned around to see Michael standing before me, looking handsome as ever.

"I feel like I haven't seen you in years," he said, sympathetically cocking his head to the side.

"Well, here I am. I'm here, and ready to fail this exam," I said, hoping to mask my melancholy with sarcasm.

I looked straight up at him and met his gaze. Even through my somber state, he could still make me weak in the knees. A feeling I would usually resent because of my relationship with Nicholas, I suddenly felt grateful for. I was grateful for any feeling that wasn't pain.

"Let's all get a drink afterwards," he offered. Before I could reject the offer, Alex materialized out of nowhere and chimed in.

He threw his arm around my shoulders and shook me a little bit. "Mike, did you say drinks?" Alex turned me around so I could face him. "Hastings, you're alive! And you've given yourself a make-over!"

I had no energy for a quick retort.

"Yeah, you, me, Amalia, and Olivia, drinks after the midterm. I'm not taking no for an answer," Michael replied.

"Please take your seats," a loud voice boomed, following by feedback on the loudspeaker.

"Sure, guys. I'll be there," I said, begrudgingly.

I made my way over to the first available seat, which just so happened to be next to Michael. He gave me a warm, reassuring smile that translated to "Everything is going to be fine." I smiled back and secretly wished I could believe him.

Chapter 9

Fifth Avenue

Nicholas,
You're gone. Not a moment has passed in the two weeks we have been apart that I haven't thought of you. It doesn't make sense. Nothing makes sense anymore.
Amalia

I never sent it.

Before I knew it, the week was over and it was Friday, the day before the big NYU dinner that Liz insisted I attend. That afternoon, I had agreed to meet Cassandra for coffee and dress-shopping.

Cassandra always had a way of making me feel better. When we were in high school she was crowned Homecoming Queen, and President of the Student Organization. I'm pretty sure I was crowned "Class Nobody," or maybe that was just a self-proclaimed title.

"You have to arrive looking fabulous!" she stated when she called me this morning.

I unwillingly agreed and also rationalized that nothing I owned fit me anymore, and I needed to go clothes shopping anyway. I checked my phone; it was now two-twenty, twenty minutes later than we had agreed to meet. She was late once again. Thank God for smartphones, I thought as I pulled up an article from *The Huffington Post* on my cell.

I looked up just as Cassandra burst through the door. "I'm so sorry! Big meeting, client was late, need coffee now," she said as she plopped down onto the stool.

"It's not a big deal, besides you gave me time to do some reading," I said, switching my phone to vibrate. "Just don't make a habit of it. You don't want to end up one of those Manhattan women who are completely obsessed with their jobs and lose all of their friends."

"Never!"

"Good," I smiled. "I'd miss you too much."

"Speaking of work, do you have lot of school work to catch up on?" she asked.

I had barely done any work for school during the past two weeks and the workload was really piling up. I did decently on my midterm, but there was definitely room for improvement. It was to the point where any free moment I acquired had to be spent doing school work.

"Um, it's a lot of work but I will get it done," I answered.

We grabbed our coffees to-go, and headed to Saks Fifth Avenue. I wasn't greatly interested in shopping like most women were, but even I had to admire the beautifully decorated, prestigious department store. I glanced down at my Converse sneakers and wondered if it were possible to be under-dressed to go shopping. Being that Cassandra worked for a well-known fashion magazine, she had an in with nearly every major department school in Manhattan.

"Cassandra, my love!" said a voice from behind us. "John! *Come va?*" Cassandra said, returning his enthusiasm and throwing in a little Italian.

I turned around to be greeted by a tall, thin, very handsome man. I noticed his outfit and decided I was definitely underdressed. He was wearing black dress pants, a light-blue fitted button-down with the sleeves rolled up, and a navy-blue silk tie to pull it all together.

"*Molto bene*, Cassandra! Who is your enchanting friend?"

"Amalia," she said, beaming. She pointed to me and then pointed to him. "This is John. He's one of the sales associates here and a dear friend of mine."

"Great to meet you," I offered a small smile and extended my hand for a handshake. It seemed like a handshake-worthy situation.

One hour, and two glasses of complementary champagne later, I made my way to the register to purchase my brand-new, little black, three-hundred- dollar Nanette Lepore cocktail dress. I didn't know if it was the store, the champagne, or the nervous breakdown I had been experiencing lately, but spending three hundred on a dress I'd only wear once seemed like a great idea.

I turned to Cassie, who was typing away on her phone. "Thank you for the day out, this is exactly what I needed. I almost felt like my old self today."

She looked up from what she was doing, smiled brightly and gave me a hug. "You deserve to be happy, sweetie, and that's why," she paused for effect. "This dress is on me."

I starred at her, stunned. "No! Absolutely not, there is no way I could ever accept something this expensive from you. Please, forget about it."

I playfully tried to grab the dress from her, but she continued to resist.

"Stop it!" she laughed, holding her up her hand for emphasis. "It's my pleasure. This is the first time I've seen a smile on your face in weeks. Besides, they're going to give me a huge discount anyway because they're terrified of my boss."

It was true. Cassandra worked directly under the Editor in Chief of her magazine, one ill word from Cassie about her shopping experience to her boss and the store would essentially be blacklisted.

"Wear it well and have fun tomorrow," she said as she grabbed her purse and coat.

I watched with great delight as Cassie pulled out her American

Express Gold card and charged the dress.

"Thank you for everything, you truly are a wonderful friend," I said and hugged her one last time before she walked up to the register. I sat back down on the large white couch outside of the dressing room and spread my arms across the back of it. I could feel the tension leaving my shoulders, and only wished I had an ottoman to put my feet up on.

"More champagne, Miss Hastings?" John said.

I let out a soft laugh and said, "Sure. What the hell."

Chapter 10

Space between us

When I arrived downtown at the The Millennium Hilton for the dinner the next night, the first person to greet me was Olivia. I was stunned by her appearance. She was wearing a low-cut, dark-burgundy-colored dress, with three-inch Christian Louboutin heels. She had traded in her usual tight pony tail for long loose waves, and the clear lip gloss was replaced by a bright-red pout. This transformation was huge, when compared with her usual dowdy and antiquated appearance. Tonight she gave Audrey Hepburn a run for her money.

"You look absolutely stunning, Olivia," I said. "Did you come with a date?"

"No. I, um, didn't come with anyone," she said, her voice shaking a bit.

I realized that my staring was probably making her uncomfortable, so I turned my gaze to the dining room. Even from far away, I could see the flickering candles on each numbered table.

"Let's get inside, It's a little cold in this hallway," I shivered. It had grown uncomfortably cold outside. Fall had come and gone as a fast blur. It was now December tenth, a mere ten days until the last day of Winter semester, and fifteen days until Christmas. I suddenly had a sullen thought; this would be my first Christmas without a boyfriend in years. I shook my head, determined not to let my thoughts of Nicholas plague me tonight.

"I have to go say hello to someone," Olivia said. "Will you be alright by yourself?"

I was beginning to feel like a charity project. Ever since my break-up, my friends had been handling me with kid gloves.

"Of course," I nodded, trying to sound as convincing as possible. "Go see your friend."

A busboy came around, offering **hors d'oeuvres and champagne. I took the opportunity to get some food in my system, and grab some bubbly.** I wasn't alone for long. A few minutes later, Liz found me. She was wearing a long midnight-blue colored dress, with small black kitten heels. She had her long red hair pulled back into a bun exposing elegant pearl earrings, a look I deemed very uncharacteristic of her. I guess we're all playing dress-up tonight, I thought.

"Thank you for coming, you look amazing," was all she said to me.

Before I could open my mouth to return the compliment, she was halfway across the room, greeting someone else. I looked around the beautifully decorated dining room and recognized a lot of people from NYU. I had to hand it to them. Liz, and the rest of the alumni committee, had done a wonderful job organizing this party.

"Amalia?" a voice from behind me asked. I turned around to see Michael standing before me, holding two glasses of champagne.

Dressed in a classic black suit, crisp white dress shirt underneath, and no tie, he was by far the most attractive man in the room.

He handed me a glass. "You look so beautiful, I almost didn't recognize you."

I smiled and made a mental note to further thank Cassandra for the new dress. Although, I wasn't exactly sure if that was a compliment or not, but I was trying to keep positive.

"There seems to be a lot of that going around tonight," I said.

"I barely recognized my class mates without text books attached to their arms."

He let out a warm laugh, raised his glass to me, and we toasted. Out of the corner of my eye, I noticed Olivia talking passionately to a man. She was waving her arms at him, dramatically driving her point home. Unfortunately, his back was toward me, and I couldn't see who it was, but the conversation definitely seemed heated.

"Who is Olivia talking to?" I asked. Michael turned around and looked in their direction. "I can't tell", he said, squinting his eyes.

Olivia grabbed the mystery man by the suit jacket and led him out into the hotel lobby, nearly knocking over two chairs in the process. Michael turned back to me, eyes widened.

"Well, she certainly seems to be able to handle herself," he said with a laugh.

"Yeah, wow!" I said, us both laughing. "Who knew she had it in her?"

In unison, Michael and I took a sip of our champagne and turned toward the dance floor. Even through the noisy guests I could hear "Begin Again" by Taylor Swift playing over the speakers, and one by one couples started making their way toward the dance floor. Taylor Swift was one of my favorite artists and happily this was one of the few songs by her that I could listen to without automatically regressing back into depression.

"I love this song," I whispered.

Suddenly, Michael took the champagne flute out of my hand and placed it on a nearby table.

"What are you doing?" I asked suddenly feeling very nervous. My dance moves began and ended with The Locomotion.

"*I'm* not doing anything. *We're* dancing," he said, as he took my arm.

The only time I had slow-danced with a man was at my younger brother's Bar Mitzvah seven years ago, with my high-school boyfriend. I spent half of the night stepping on his feet until he finally got so fed up that he refused to ever dance with me again.

The thought that Michael and I would have a similar experience fueled me to stop him.

"No," I answered quickly. "I'm sorry." I shook my head and tried to back away.

Michael took a step back and pretended to be offended.

"I mean, not *no*, I don't not want to dance with you, per se. I just don't know how to dance," I said, resisting his grasp.

Without looking at me, he said, "Then it's a good thing I do".

Before I knew it, Michael enveloped my right hand in his, and placed my left on his chest. His left hand rested lightly on my hip, and pulled me close until his face was inches away from mine. I felt a deep shiver run up my body and focused hard on my footwork. He was wearing the same cologne he'd had on the day in class when he leaned close to me and I could feel the familiar flush of blood rushing to my cheeks. I did my best to ignore it, and decided I had better focus on what we were currently doing. I didn't want to be remembered as the twenty-three-year-old weirdo who can't dance for the rest of my time at this school.

A few seconds passed and we were dancing flawlessly. I looked around the floor and saw everyone I knew from school dressed up, looking elegant and refined. I couldn't help but allow a smile to creep onto my lips. I could get used to a life like this.

"Listen, I heard what happened with Nicholas," he said, softly.

I stopped dancing and let go of his hand.

"How did you know?" I asked. "I haven't really spoken to that many people about it".

I wondered why he had to bring this up and ruin our perfect moment.

"Alex told me," he answered with a shrug. "I was asking around if anyone had seen or spoken to you lately, and he told me you were too upset to come to class. I was going to come visit you, but I couldn't remember your address".

For a moment, I was utterly stunned. For one thing, how did Alex know anything about my break-up? Also, did Michael say he was going to come to my apartment to essentially check on me?

"How does Alex know?" I asked, genuinely confused, but my question came off more as irritated.

"I'm really sorry, I shouldn't have brought it up," he said, looking embarrassed.

He took my hand back into his and resumed dancing.

"I just want you to know that if you need to talk, I've been told I'm a good listener," he said, taking the opportunity to dip me.

I started wondering if his girlfriend, Marge, was the one who granted him the title of "good listener". Or if she knew he slow-danced with other girls.

"I appreciate it, Michael," I said. "But I am more of the suffer-in-silence type."

Suddenly, Olivia angrily stormed over to us. Michael and I dropped hands immediately, preparing to be scolded for doing something wrong.

"Have you seen my phone? I can't find it," she said, frantically searching the tables.

Her eyes quickly scanned the room and she tossed tablecloths around and lifted up place settings. Finally locating her phone on the next table over, she grabbed her jacket and threw it on.

"Never mind, here it is. I'm leaving." She stormed off.

I took a step away from Michael and began to walk in her direction.

"Olivia!" I called after her, picking up the pace. "What's wrong? Where are you going?"

I started chasing her through the lobby, dodging caterers holding the plates of hors d'oeuvres. I chased her past the bell-hops and the concierge desk, and then out onto Church Street.

Why had she run out?

I was suddenly clearly aware of the harsh winter air and wished I had grabbed my coat. I walked quickly up and down the block, calling her name, but she was nowhere to be seen. The Financial District was a ghost town this time of night and it seemed as though she had virtually disappeared. Feeling defeated, I decided to give up and go back inside, when I felt a hand on mine pull me around. I signed with relief and unclenched. I felt relieved that I had found her, but when we stood face to face, I saw that it wasn't Olivia, it was Michael.

Still holding my hand, he pulled me closer, this time not leaving any space between us. He ran his hand down my back, then through my hair, and then over my lips. I stood frozen in a mixture of fear and ecstasy as he rested his hand under my neck and passionately pushed his lips onto mine.

As I felt his mouth come crashing down onto mine, I realized I had wanted this all along. I wanted it from the first moment I met him, even when I had a boyfriend, even before I really knew it. A large part of me had always wanted Michael. I should have been happy, should have pushed him into a cab and made out with him feverishly in the back seat until we finally arrived at my apartment, but I didn't. Instead, I stopped him.

"I'm sorry, Michael. I just can't," I said, pushing him off of me.

I felt my face turn about three different shades of red, but I was too mortified to see what his face was doing. I couldn't confront him. I felt a myriad feelings as I turned abruptly and following in Olivia's footsteps, ran down the street until I reached the nearest subway.

Chapter 11

The morning after

The next day I woke up feeling a haunting mixture of panic and regret. Panic, because tomorrow I would have to go to class and face Michael, all while keeping my composure. Drawing any outside attention to the situation would be terrible for both of us.

Regret, because even though Michael had a girlfriend, even though I was still hopelessly in love with Nicholas, and even though it was utterly and entirely wrong, I wanted to kiss him again. Of course, there was the possibility that he and Marge had broken up, or maybe he had every intention of breaking up with her but couldn't wait any longer to be with me. Maybe the sheer force of our kiss broke whatever spell she had him under and now he was irrevocably in love with me. Unfortunately, my puerile post-make-out, freak-out, likely insured that another kiss would never happen again. I had blown my chance and it was all I could think about on this gray and rainy morning after. I decided to stay in bed and let the stupidity of my actions wash over me.

Monday.
I took extra time getting ready that morning, carefully choosing an outfit, gingerly applying my eye make-up, all in an effort to delay the inevitable as much as possible. The inevitable being the

awkward and discomfiting encounter I was going to have with Michael in about thirty-five minutes. I put on the finishing touches of my ensemble, including my favorite pair of knee-high boots. I grabbed my hideous over-sized purse that fits all of my books, and headed out into the penetrating cold.

Even though it was freezing outside, I still opted to walk the few blocks from my apartment to Washington Place. The brisk air was helping at least. Even in the distance, I could see the giant arch, guarding over Washington Square Park. It was still, to this day, my favorite landmark in Manhattan. The Chrysler Building was a close second.

When I arrived at school, I spotted Alex outside. I felt a wave of panic wash over me.

He was standing outside of the building, frantically looking around and smoking a cigarette. I walked extra slowly past a crowd of undergrads who were laughing and passing out flyers for a local bar. I felt a wave of jealously of the simplicity of their lives.

Just as I put my hand on the door, he spotted me.

"Hastings!" he said, giving me a small wave. He motioned for me to come closer.

He must know about me and Michael. After all, why else would he be waiting for me outside the building with that anxious look on his face? He was going to berate me about the kiss.

"What's going on, Alex?" I asked innocently. "You look a little peaked, is everything alright?"

He nodded his head and dropped the cigarette onto the floor, not even bothering to step on it.

"You know we get our midterm grades back today, Hastings?"

Wow, I thought. This day just got a lot worse.

"Right, I completely forgot. Our final is next class too, isn't it?" I asked, still wondering why he had that sullen look on his face.

"Yeah it is," he said, blowing off the question.

I checked my watched and realized if I didn't leave now, I would be late.

"Hey, have you seen or spoken to Olivia at all?" he asked, not maintaining eye contact.

"No," I shook my head. "I haven't." I was convinced that he couldn't look me in the eye because Michael had told him what happened. "Not since she stormed out of the dinner party that you missed on Saturday".

"No," he replied curtly. "I was there."

"I'm sorry, I didn't see you," I said, now even more freaked. "I, um, have to go inside and use the ladies' room before class. I'll see you in there".

I scrambled up the two flights of stairs, too anxious to wait for the elevator, and dodged into the restroom. I checked under the stalls; no one was there. I was in the clear.

Crap, Alex was at the dance! Michael didn't tell him anything, he saw it himself! I took long, deep relaxing breaths that I had learned one summer while taking Tai Chi, and ordered myself to calm down. Maybe Alex hadn't seen us; maybe he was just being his usual quirky self and his mood had nothing to do with me whatsoever. I mean, after all, not everything's about me, right?

The bathroom door opened and two girls from class walked in. I let out a soft sigh, and one of the girls turned around and gave me a dirty look, I then decided I had to go into class. Luckily, I saw Olivia right away and scrambled to get the seat next to her.

"Hey, I just saw Alex outside," I said, determined to talk about anything, or anyone, other than Michael. "He was asking about you."

"Oh well he's going to see me when he comes in, so I guess if he has something to say to me, he can say it then," she answered, flipping through the pages of her notebook.

She didn't appear to be distracted, more like she was ignoring me.

"Um, Olivia, is everything alright?" I asked, now fearing that she knew the truth as well.

"Of course, Amalia," she answered, still not looking up. "Why wouldn't I be alright?"

"Well you kind of darted out of the NYU dinner on Saturday and apparently no one has heard from you since," I answered, looking straight at her.

She finally looked up and met my gaze.

"It was nothing. A family thing, that's all," she said, and finally gave me a small smile. Still smiling, she looked past me and said, "Hey, Michael."

I quickly turned around, knocking my books and pen on the floor.

"Let me get that for you," he started to bend down.

"I got it!" I said, much more loudly than intended. "I mean, don't worry about it. I'm the klutz, not you. Go find a seat, really it's fine."

I knew I was rambling, but I couldn't stop. My nerves were in overdrive, and it didn't help that he'd come to class that morning looking perfect. I felt as if the universe was punishing me. I did something bad; I kissed another girl's boyfriend. Well, actually, he kissed me. Either way, the universe was not pleased.

"Just wanted to say hello, ladies," I heard him utter.

"Oh, hey," I turned to say, but he was gone.

I watched as Michael made his way to the back of the classroom and found an empty seat near Alex. The two of them would undoubtedly be talking about me and Olivia and our matching tantrums on Saturday night. Still being ignored by Olivia, I sank lower into my seat, hoping that today's class would go by quickly.

Chapter 12

Story Tease

"How did you do on your midterm?" Cassandra asked, adding Splenda to her skimmed latte.

"I don't want to talk about it."

I hadn't seen Cassie since the day she bought me the dress for the now-infamous NYU dinner. So when she asked me to meet her after work for coffee at Financier, I couldn't say no.

"So Cassandra, what would you say if I told you that something happened?" I twirled the spoon around in my coffee.

"That's pretty cryptic, Amy. What do you mean by 'something'?" she said, only half-listening as she typed with her perfectly manicured nails on her phone.

I thought back to the days in high school, before everyone I knew had a cell phone, when you had to call someone's house and hope they would be home to take your call, and then place your trust in their brother, or mother, that they would relay the message that you called back to you. Those days, when I wanted to talk to my best friend about something important, I could rely on her to give me her undivided attention, not ignore me on the go with the latest smartphone application. Desperate to regain her attention, I decided to come right out with it. I looked around the coffee shop, even though we were down in Tribeca, I wanted to make sure no one from school was around to witness what was sure to be an epic freak-out.

I looked right at Cassandra, who still had her head down. "Michael and I kissed."

Cassandra dropped her phone onto the table and pushed her chair back. "You what?" she cried. "Amalia Danette Hastings! You little hussy! I can't believe you kissed him."

I sat there calmly sipping my coffee, which only made her react more alarmingly.

"Oh no," I said, now smiling with amusement. "He kissed me. At the dinner last Saturday night."

Cassandra looked as if she had been hit in the gut. It was clear by her shocked demeanor that she never actually thought Michael and I would hook up.

She pulled her chair back in and leaned over the table. She ran hands over her skirt and composed herself.

"So, how was it?" she asked, eyes wide with anticipation.

"How was what?" I asked, enjoying her attention a little too much.

She looked around the room, suddenly aware that we were still downtown and not too far from my school.

"How was he, you know, in bed?" she asked, grinning. She raised an eyebrow and bit her bottom lip, desperate for details.

Now it was my turn to get excited. I held my head in my hands and forcefully pushed the hair away from my face.

"Woah! Cassie, I didn't sleep with him. He kissed me outside of the hotel and I sort of freaked out and ran away," I said, slightly embarrassed by reliving the experience.

Cassie just looked at me; the smile had vanished from her face and was replaced by a grimace.

"This story is terrible," she folded her arms. "I'm really disappointed in you. I got all excited for nothing. You know what you are? A story tease."

I sat back in my chair and let out an exasperated sigh. I put my left hand on my forehead and shook my head at her. "Listen missy, number one, Michael has a girlfriend. Number two, I am still not over Nick, and number three," I said as I checked my watch. "I have to get to Brooklyn and meet him and Olivia, to study for our final, which is in two days."

Without saying another word, I got up, threw my paper coffee cup into the trash and grabbed my heavy down coat.

"Fine. Goodbye Amalia 'story tease' Hastings, I shall talk to you tomorrow," she said, returning to her iPhone.

I arrived at Olivia's Park Slope apartment right on time, hoping to beat Michael there, but there he was sitting at her kitchen table, ready to work. It was official. It was impossible for the guy to not look good. Olivia was back to her usual dowdy self, wearing jeans that were a size or two too big, and an oversized NYU sweatshirt with a picture of a Bobcat on it that she undoubtedly purchased at orientation from the school bookstore. The two of them looked as if they were already down to business and I was interrupting. There were index cards spread out all over the table, two different Cognitive Neuroscience text books, and a worn-out copy of the Gray's Anatomy.

"Coffee?" Olivia asked, holding a fresh pot in one hand and a mug in the other.

"Sure," I replied quickly, even though I was still a little wired from my last cup.

I pulled my long blonde hair into a tight pony tail to get it off my face, in an attempt to show that I too was ready to work. Even if Michael's presence was a distraction. I had only been there two minutes and I already felt butterflies in my stomach. A few curls fell out of place, and I quickly tucked them behind my ears.

Over the next two hours, the three of us had two more cups of coffee, polished off a pizza, and managed to cover nearly every ounce of material that was going to be on our final. Olivia's phone rang and she retrieved the call in her bedroom, leaving Michael and me alone. Why did he have to look so damn sexy?

Up until now I actually managed to compose myself in what I thought was a normal manner, but now that we were alone I felt all of my anxiety return. He must have noticed it because he moved his chair closer to me and said, "Everything alright?"

I couldn't look at him. I told myself to keep my eyes in the book and to not engage.

Quickly I answered, "I'm just not entirely understanding this last chapter," as I flipped through the pages of my notebook, pretending to read.

"Well, I think by now I know this stuff backwards and forwards, so if you'd like I can come by tomorrow after work and we can get in one more cram session before the exam," he offered.

"You mean, come by my apartment?" I asked, horrified.

"Yes," he let out a soft laugh. "I mean, if that's a problem we can go somewhere else."

"No, it's not a problem. Why would it be a problem?" I rambled.

"Great, so I'll come by around seven and we can hit the books. There's just one more thing, Amalia."

"Yes," I said, eyes widened. I wondered if he was going to say we needed to talk about what happened last weekend.

"I need you to tell me your address again, because I forgot where you live".

"Right!" I laughed nervously. I could feel my face turning red. "Of course you need my address. I live on the corner of West 10th and Greenwich Street. It's a brown building; you can't miss it."

"Perfect. It's getting pretty late so I'm going to take off," he said grabbing his coat. "I'll see you tomorrow."

Just as Michael closed the door behind him, Olivia reappeared from her bedroom.

"Where did Michael go?" she asked, cleaning up our empty coffee mugs.

"He had to go home," I said, trying to sound cavalier. "He has work early tomorrow morning."

Olivia nodded and returned to cleaning. Relief rolled through me; she was obviously unaware as to what was going on between Michael and me, and I had gotten nervous for nothing the other day.

"So who was on the phone?" I asked.

"What?" she asked, as if she was confused by my question.

I glared back at her. "Olivia, you were just on the phone for about fifteen minutes. Who were you talking to?"

"Oh, um, my mom. You know how it is, living on my own now. She calls a lot." Olivia walked back into the kitchen, turned on the dishwasher, and started looking out the window. She was acting fine up until now; I was reminded of her actions in class the other day, when I thought she was mad at me. I wondered if something was going on with her family. She obviously didn't want to talk about it, and I took the hint that she wanted me to leave. I put on my coat, collected my things, and walked over to Olivia. I reached over and put my hand on her shoulder.

I put on my coat, collected my things and crossed to her. I reached over and put my hand on her shoulder. "Olivia, if something is bothering you and you need to talk about it, I just want you to know I am here for you."

She turned around and gave me an unexpected hug.

"Thank you," she said, still holding on to me. "Really, I'm fine, just worried about this test!" she released me and lightly hit me with a dish towel.

Suddenly, it dawned on me. The clandestine phone call, her random bad moods, the mystery man at the dinner, and any excuse to change the topic of conversation, it was suddenly crystal-clear. Her back was to me, still cleaning her already-pristine counter tops. I playfully tapped her on the shoulder.

"So, Olivia, who is he?" I asked with a wide-knowing grin.

"Who?" she asked, refusing to meet my eyes.

"Your mystery boyfriend!" I cried. "Come on, Olivia, you've been acting crazy since the dinner party so spill the beans already and tell me who he is!"

Well that certainly got her attention. She whipped around, nearly knocking all of her freshly washed dishes onto the floor, and stared back at me with wide eyes. "How did you know?"

How *did* I know? Maybe it was because I too was in the middle of a secret romance, or at least I hoped to be, and I recognized some of the signs. I considered telling her about Michael, and then maybe she and I could compare notes. I chickened out, and instead went for a more sophomoric answer.

"I know, because I'm a girl," I said. I figured she would accept that reasoning.

"Please, Amalia, don't say anything to anyone!" she said looking really anxious. "You're right, it is a secret, and I am not ready for our entire circle to get a hold of this information".

I knew exactly how she felt, so all I said was, "Of course."

She gave me another hug as I glanced at the clock on her microwave and figured I had better get going. As I made my way into the elevator, I felt proud of myself for figuring out the reason for Olivia's erratic behavior. I knew first hand that love certainly can make you act crazy. When I got outside, it was snowing. It was the first snowfall of the season and I was reminded that Christmas Eve was in a few days. I pulled my faux fur-rimmed hood tightly over my head and began to make my way home.

Chapter 13

Crossing the line

It was now 6:45, a mere fifteen minutes prior to Michael's arrival and Christina still had not departed from our apartment. I could have sworn she told me she was going out to dinner with her boyfriend tonight and staying at his place, and that she would be leaving around 6:30. Calm down, I told myself; she's probably just running late. I didn't want her to still be here when he arrived; I imagined it could be a very awkward encounter if she were to exit while he was entering. I'd have to explain where she was going, in an effort to make Michael feel like I didn't kick her out in anticipation of our "study session."

I felt a wave of relief wash over me when she called out, "I'm leaving, see you tomorrow!" and heard the door slam.

I ran back into my bedroom and looked myself up and down in my full-length mirror. Hair straight? Check. New "casual-looking but still effortlessly beautiful" outfit? Check. Natural make-up? Check. I had to look good without it being obvious I was trying to look good. After all, we were just going to be sitting around in my apartment; I couldn't exactly put on a ball gown. I smacked on a final coat of lip-gloss and nearly jumped out of my skin when I heard the buzzer go off. I took a deep breath, walked over to my door and buzzed him in. I had about two minutes while he rode the elevator to plant myself on the couch and pretend I had been studying this entire time. A short eternity later, I heard a knock on my door.

"It's open!" I called out, trying not to sound too desperate.

Finally, he had arrived, fully prepared to study, with more index cards, two study guides that companioned our text books, and to my surprise two cups of Starbucks coffee. I jumped off the couch to give him a hand, but he swatted me away, dumping everything into a pile on my table.

"One soy Vanilla Latte for you," he said handing me the to-go cup. "And a half caff, no foam, extra shot of mocha, skim macchiato for me".

"Oh really? That's what you ordered?" I asked with a sarcastic smile.

"Sure," he answered, smiling. "What's the problem?" He raised one sexy eyebrow.

I put my coffee on the table, took his out of his hand. "Well then you won't mind if I try some?"

"Please, by all means," he offered with a serious face.

I took a sip and nearly spit the sludge out.

"Ew! This coffee is black, and it doesn't even have any sugar in it!"

"Oh right. I always get black coffee and macchiatos mixed up," he took a sip of his disgusting coffee.

"That's appalling," I said playfully as I stacked all of our books into a neat pile.

"Well, thank you for the surprise cup of joe," I said honestly. "But shouldn't we get started? I thought we could start with the most recent chapter and work our way backwards to the beginning of the semester."

"Sure thing." he said complacently. "I am merely here to help".

Over the next two hours we hit the books hard, studying every morsel of information given to us over the past few months. I was even able to regurgitate most of it when Michael tested me from the make-shift flash cards he brought over.

"I don't know about you, but I can sure use a break," he said as he rubbed his eyes.

I nodded in agreement and let out a soft sigh. "Do you want anything? Maybe something to drink?"

"Ugh. I'd love a glass of wine if you have it."

"Well Michael Rathbourne!" I dramatically paced a hand to my chest. "Drinking on a school night? That doesn't seem at all like something we do at all." I shook my head, pretending to scold him.

He offered me a soft laugh as I opened a new bottle of Cabernet and poured us both a much-needed glass. I handed the goblet over to him and we toasted.

"To acing our final!" he declared, holding the wine glass high.

I let out a small laugh. "I'll definitely drink to that."

As the evening went on, I started to feel a little more comfortable. I don't know if it was the wine or the conversation, but I felt like we were really hitting it off. Dare I say in a romantic way? My heart fluttered quickly as we sat on the couch and talked about school, our friends, and even our families.

"Can I ask you something?" He said, narrowing his eyes.

"Sure," I answered, feeling my heart beat harder.

"Not that it's any of my business, but how do you pay for this apartment?" he asked, moving a little bit closer to me.

"Oh. Well, it's kind of embarrassing," I said, suddenly feeling very warm. "I took out extra student loans and put them towards the rent of the apartment. I just really wanted to live here and it seemed like a good idea at the time, but I'm definitely not going to do it next year. Also, my parents help me out. Just a little, though!"

"Hey listen, it's really expensive living in this city," he offered, easing my insecurity. "I mean this isn't Gossip Girl, none of us are ridiculously rich. Except maybe Alex. I think he might be rich."

"I have no idea," I said, straightening my posture and looking directly into his eyes.

I leaned a little closer, hoping he would take the hint and kiss me.

"So what are your holiday plans?" He sipped his second glass of wine.

My shoulders deflated and I sank back into the couch.

"My mother is an atheist and my father is Jewish, so for the most part we don't really celebrate the winter holidays in my house. I usually spend Christmas with my friend Cassandra's family."

The truth was I loved spending Christmas with her. I was a part of something the entire world got to enjoy, while my family devotedly protested against it.

"That sounds like a great time. I've only met her a few times, but she seems like a nice girl." He gave me a small smile. "You're lucky to have such a good friend that you can spend the holidays with."

"Yeah, I guess," I said. "She's definitely a good friend." Cassandra was lucky to have such a kind and welcoming family.

"What about you?" I asked, fluffing my hair up a bit. "Do you go home to see your family?"

"I actually convinced my parents to come into the city and spend Christmas here this year," he said. "It's going to be nice to not have to travel for once, and this way I can take them and maybe even go ice-skating in Bryant Park."

"What about your sister? How are you all going to fit in your apartment?"

"She's spending the holidays with her boyfriend," he explained. "They're getting pretty serious; I wouldn't be surprised if he popped the question this weekend."

Hearing this news, I couldn't help but wonder how serious he and Marge were, or if they were even still together. I leaned back onto the couch, loving how easy this was. Just to sit here and be with him felt perfect. I took another sip of my wine and made a secret wish that he felt the same way.

It struck me as odd he hadn't brought up our kiss at the hotel, but I certainly wasn't going to be the one to say something. I looked up from the spread of textbooks on my table, and caught Michael's eye. He had been staring at me. I suddenly felt self-conscious, as if I had something in my teeth and he was too polite to point it out. He took the wine glass out of my hand and placed it on the coffee table. Before I could say a word, he roped his fingers through my hair and pulled me in. He started kissing my mouth, lightly biting my lips at first, then passionately pushing me down onto the couch. I could taste the wine on his lips. He positioned himself on top of me and ran his hand down my stomach, and then down the back of my leg. I kissed back, hard and fast, like someone who was eating a meal they were scared would be taken away. He backed up off of me and a pit of disappointment opened in my stomach.

"No, don't stop," I uttered, but in my head it sounded more like a plea.

Michael let out a low breathy laugh. In seconds, he picked me up and carried me through the hallway into my bedroom. Thank goodness no one was home. He sat on my bed and effortlessly placed me on top of him. I was always amazed at how strong men were; how they could whip you around like little dolls without breaking a sweat.

I used the opportunity of facing him to unbutton his shirt, while still afraid to stop kissing. He returned the motion by carefully pulling my chocolate-brown sweater over my head. Next came my pants, then his pants, my bra and underwear, and then we were crossing the line between friends and lovers.

Chapter 14

Baby Buddha

I woke up the next morning like I would any other. I got out of bed, put on my slippers, and stumbled into the bathroom. It wasn't until I caught a glimpse of myself in the mirror that I finally put the pieces of last night's indiscretion into place. My curly hair had metamorphosed into a blonde weave of bird's nest-esque tangles, looking even wilder than the usual bedhead I sported in the morning. My lips were raw and cracked from hours of kissing. My blue eyes were entirely red from only five short hours of sleep. I also had a small but undeniable headache from the wine, and my thigh muscles were aching from sitting on top of Michael for so long.

Problems I was more than happy to have.

The events of last night had accelerated quickly, and after round two, Michael had to say goodnight. He didn't end up leaving until after one in the morning, part of the reason I looked like a New York Doll. I walked into my kitchen to make urgently needed coffee. I couldn't help but hum to myself as I cleaned out the coffee pot. In the midst of my bliss, I noticed he had left his gloves on my table. Before I forgot, I brought them into my room and tucked them into the inside pocket of my purse.

I walked, or maybe it was a skip, back into the kitchen to

continue making breakfast, and nearly jumped out of my skin when I saw Christina standing there.

"Oh my gosh, I had no idea you were home!" I cried. "You scared the crap out of me."

"I'm sorry!" she said. "Yeah, I came home about an hour ago. I have to go to class at ten today."

"Me too," I said as I looked at the clock; it was only 8:45, plenty of time to get ready for class. "So you said you came home this morning right? Not last night," I asked as I filled the kettle up with water.

"Yup," was all she said, as she walked out of the kitchen and claimed the first shower.

I didn't mind. She could have the first shower for the rest of the month and I wouldn't mind. I sat on my couch and happily sipped my coffee and ate my English muffin. Nothing was going to ruin my good mood; not today.

Another cup of coffee and a quick shower later, I was off to class to take my final. I had arrived at ten o'clock on the dot and to my dismay, the only available seat was next to Alex. I looked around the room for Michael and spotted him in the second row, deeply engrossed in his study cards.

"Damn, I need a cocktail." Alex slumped in his seat.

I rolled my eyes at him. "It's ten o'clock in the morning, man. Get it together."

He didn't bother to answer.

I took out two black-ink pens, and my reading glasses for good measure. I sat patiently as the teacher's assistant passed out the blue test booklets.

"You have one hour," the T.A. said. He wrote down the current time and the time the test would end on the chalkboard.

Thankfully, the studying had actually paid off and I breezed through the test in a record twenty-five minutes. I watched as a few students, with relieved looks on their faces, made their way to the front of the class and placed their booklets on the desk.

I wanted to time my departure around Michael's but he still appeared to be writing, so I walked up to the front. On my way out, I glanced back at Michael. I wondered if we would get a chance to talk later today.

I started to make my way down the stairs when Olivia called my name.

"Amalia, wait up!" I turned around as she quickly made her way down the stairs.

"Hey! Wow how about that final? I definitely failed. She twisted her hair into a tight bun. "Do you want to grab some lunch?"

"Sure, I guess," I said wondering if she had only studied the one time I came over. "Let's drown our memories of this test in Chinese food."

We hailed a cab to Washington Street and made our way to Baby Buddha, my favorite downtown Chinese food restaurant. We were seated immediately and set up with our own teapot, duck sauce, and those delicious crunchies they give you that I never did learn the proper name for. After only three minutes of sitting, a young, delicately framed girl with long jet-black hair appeared at our table. The service was extremely quick for that time of day, and after a quick glance of the menu we decided on the vegetable dumplings and fried rice for Olivia and me to share. I sat eating my crunchies, listening to Olivia complain about how difficult the final had been.

After my second cup of tea, I started feeling weird about what happened between Michael and me. We hadn't spoken or technically seen each other since last night. I wondered if he thought sex was a huge mistake and was going to avoid me now. What if he was too ashamed to ever speak to me again? Or maybe I was using him to hide my own pain, my breakup with Nicholas.

I suddenly couldn't take the anxiety any more. Keeping this secret to myself was killing me and it wouldn't hurt just to tell someone.

"Olivia, I have to tell you something." I put down the now-empty bowl of crunchies. "But before I tell you, you have to promise me you aren't going to tell anyone."

She looked up from her dish confused but welcoming. "Amalia, I promise. Is everything all right? Are you in some sort of trouble?"

"No, nothing like that." I shook my head and allowed myself a small laugh. "It's just something complicated and it involves Michael."

I tried to play it off like it was nothing, but by the look on her face she wasn't buying it. She waved her hand, signaling me to continue. I let out a heavy sigh. "Last night, Michael came over my apartment to help me study. While he was over we ended up, well, you know."

"You guys hooked up?" She had a horrified look on her face.

Suddenly I felt nauseous. Maybe this wasn't such a good idea.

"Yeah, pretty much." I nervously sipped my green tea.

She pushed her plate away from her, as if she suddenly needed more table space to understand what I had just told her. Her face twisted into a grimace and I felt a scolding coming on.

"All right, so what exactly happened?" she asked. "You two just kissed a little, right?"

I grew more uncomfortable with each question, but I had come too far to drop the subject.

"Um, no. We actually did a little more than that." I was utterly regretting my decision to tell her. Her judgmental stare pressed down on me as I fumbled my fork. I dropped the cutlery on the table and began to look around the room.

"I can't believe you did that," she muttered under her breath.

I felt a sudden urge to defend myself.

"Look, Olivia, I have feelings for Michael. It's not like I just randomly slept with him for kicks."

"Amalia, he has a girlfriend," she leaned forward in her chair. "He is cheating on his girlfriend with you. What do you think is going to happen, exactly? He's going to leave her for you?"

"Maybe he will; you don't know that he won't," I crossed my

arms. "You have no idea what's going through his mind."

She had a point. Just what did I expect to happen? And I didn't exactly have a grasp on what was going through his mind myself. But either way, I couldn't believe Olivia was acting like this, especially when I had been so understanding about her secret romance with an unknown suitor.

"What has he said?" she pushed. "Did he tell you he has feelings for you? Are you going to do it again? I mean, not for nothing, Amalia, but you're making a big mistake!"

All of her questions were starting to give me a headache. "It wasn't just me who made the mistake! He's the one who initiated everything. I can't believe you would be so judgmental, Olivia."

She just sat there and shook her head.

Her attitude was about as much as I could take for that afternoon. It was bad enough to have an inner monologue on repeat inside my head, telling me how bad I was. It was quite another to have one of my closest friends sit across the table and do it to me.

I reached into my purse to pull out my wallet and noticed Michael's gloves were still in there, which only further fueled my anger. I threw a twenty-dollar bill down on the table, looked right at Olivia and said, "I really expected something more from you, but I guess I was wrong." I held her gaze for a moment.

For a second I felt like I was overreacting and contemplated bringing up how silly this was. But I could tell by her withering stare she did not see the humor in all of this. As I kept her gaze, she just looked back at me, completely unapologetic and even challenging. Without saying another word, I collected my purse, my jacket, and whatever dignity I had left, and walked out of the restaurant.

Chapter 15

Sulking

Later that day I was halfway through *He's Just Not That Into You*, and completely through three salted caramel cupcakes from Magnolia Bakery, when my buzzer rang. I glanced at the clock on my cable box. The bold red neon numbers read 5:30. I wasn't expecting anyone, especially not at this time. Unwilling to move from my bed, I called out to Christina to answer the door. Apparently she wasn't home, so I grabbed one more cupcake, wrapped my blanket around me and made my way to the door.

"Yeah?" I grumbled into the intercom, still annoyed I had to move.

"Hello? Amalia, it's me. Buzz me up!" said Cassandra's voice through the intercom.

I hit the buzzer, unlocked my front door, and sluggishly made my way back to my bedroom. I hoped she was in the mood for a rom com, because I wasn't turning this movie off.

A few moments later, Cassandra was standing in my doorway, fresh from work, with her arms folded. She was wearing a dark-green dress with a camel-colored pea coat over it and dark-gray boots to pull the look together. I was in pajamas and had been since I had gotten home from lunch.

"Excuse me, Miss Couch Potato," she said, arms still folded.

"Just what exactly are you doing?"

I let out an exasperated sigh. I wasn't expecting any company this evening and after the fight I got into with Olivia at lunch, the last thing I needed was another one of my friends giving me unneeded sass. She stood stubbornly in the doorway, clearly not accepting my sigh as an answer.

"What does it look like? I'm sulking, Cassandra. I got into a big fight with Olivia after we took our final this afternoon and I'm upset about Michael because I have no idea what's going on with us," I finally said.

I was in no mood to talk about any of this, but she'd drag it out of me one way or another. So I conceded after a few more probing questions.

"So what did you and Olivia fight about? And what do you mean by 'you and Michael'? I thought you ran away from him after he kissed you?" She seemed genuinely confused. "Have you spoken to him?"

I couldn't lie to Cassandra any more than I could lie to Olivia. I just hoped Cassie's reaction would be more tame.

"Well," I said hesitantly. "That's not exactly the whole story, Cass." I watched in fear as her eyes grew wider. "Look, last night something happened."

I patted the spot on the bed next to me, an indication for her to come and join me. She dropped her Marc Jacobs purse on my desk and slipped off her boots. As she took a seat next to me on the bed I told her the entire story of what happened, leading all the way up to this afternoon when Olivia reprimanded me.

I expected a sturdy scolding from Cassandra as well, some sort of reminder of how bad I was. Maybe even an under-the-breath comment about how slutty I was. Instead, she moved closer to me and gave me a much-needed hug.

"Oh, Amalia! I'm here for you, girl, whatever you need," she said, reminding me why she was my best friend.

I hugged her back, longer than our usual embrace would last.

I really did need a friend right now, and hot tears burned behind my eyes. Then in the middle of our pow-wow, it occurred to me she had come by unannounced.

"So what are you doing here?" I said, composing myself. "Not that I'm not glad you stopped by, but don't you usually work until six or seven?"

She shook her head and gave a slight eye roll. Something gave me the feeling the conversation was no longer going to be about me.

"It's Bryce," she spat out, confirming my suspicions. It hurt that she immediately changed the conversation to something about her, but I decided one friend mad at me was enough and let her talk. "He's driving me crazy! He'll go days acting perfectly normal, calling, texting, and even making future plans. Then there are other days when I don't hear from him at all; it's complete radio silence. Oh! And if I initiate contact with him, he won't answer me for hours, it's so frustrating! I just had to leave work. The more I sat in front of my computer, the more tempted I was to check his Facebook page."

"Have you two spoken about where you are in your relationship? Are you two monogamous?" I asked. I rubbed my eyes in an attempt to feel more alert.

"Relationship? Ha! Please, monogamy? I have no idea." She waved her hands in the air. She always did have a flair for the dramatic. Her mouth turned into a self-deprecating grimace. "Any time I try to bring it up with him, he answers me with 'I just want to take things slow, and see how it goes.' I mean I really like him, Amalia. I just seriously don't know what to do."

I let out yet another sigh and shook my head. I took my wool blanket and threw some extra material over Cassandra. "I know exactly what you need."

It seemed like we were both in the same position.

She looked at me inquisitively and I handed her my last cupcake while directing her attention back to the movie. She happily accepted the treat and leaned back into the big stack of pillows I had created for myself. I grabbed the remote and hit play. It was right on the scene where Gigi tells Alex that he's afraid of getting hurt, and that she would never want to be like him. I found it quite fitting.

Chapter 16

White Christmas

Christmas Eve had come and so did a trip back to Staten Island. I stepped off the bus and took a look around. Cassandra's parents' house, which was located in a neighborhood called Newdorp, looked as winter-wonderful as ever. Inside was beautifully decorated with brand-new Christmas lights, shiny silver ornaments, red and green garlands, and stockings hung by the working chimney. I even had a stocking of my own. When I walked into the living room, I was immediately hit with the scent of cinnamon cookies, and the sounds of Frank Sinatra singing "White Christmas" over the stereo. I decided there and then that for the next two days, I was going to be blissfully unaware of anything going on outside of this house – which included Michael – and I was going to have a wonderful time if it killed me.

As I made my way into the kitchen, Cassandra's parents and a harem of guests greeted me, including her grandparents, a handful of aunts and uncles, and even her teacup Chihuahua Muffin, who had already made her away over to my new boots. Excited to get the day going, I said my hellos, dropped off my bottle of wine in the kitchen and made my way up the stairs to Cassandra's bedroom.

"You're here!" she said, dropping a half-wrapped present onto the floor.

Cassandra's childhood bedroom was about twice the size of my bedroom in the city. The walls were still painted light purple from when she was a child, but I noticed her old bedside tables were replaced with new, shiny silver ones holding up square vases packed with sunflowers.

"Are you seriously still wrapping gifts?" I asked with a smirk. It's more of an accusation than a question; she always waits until the last minute. "Did you even wrap my gift yet?"

"Oh shut up." She tossed a small, beautifully wrapped present my way.

I caught it one-handed and gave myself a mental pat on the back. I dug into the bottomless pit that is my purse and pulled out her gift. I made my way over to her bed and sat down, careful not to disturb any of the half-wrapped gifts.

"Do you realize this is my fifth consecutive year spending Christmas with you?" I handed her an envelope.

"So is this a Christmas present or an anniversary present?" she raised an eyebrow.

"Just open it!" I said as I began to rip through wrapping paper.

I carefully unwrapped the gold and green paper and was immediately blown away by the box. In bold black letters, the prestigious word *Chanel* was written in graceful script. I quickly decided it must be a joke, a re-used box she had lying around, and upon opening this box I would find yet another smaller box and so on, kind of like a Russian stacking doll. To my surprise, I did not find another box. However, what was inside was a small black patent-leather wallet with the *Chanel* insignia proudly displayed in the middle. It was the most gorgeous thing I had ever seen, and easily above the most expensive thing I owned.

"Cassandra, I cannot accept this! Honestly it's just too much. I think you need to take it back." I held it out to her.

I meant every word, but I still secretly hoped she would tell me I was being ridiculous and that of course I could take it. Which, she did, thankfully.

I jumped up and down and held the wallet over my head like a trophy. After my victory dance, I gently placed it down on the bed and ran over to give her a hug.

"Your gift definitely destroys the fifty-dollar gift card to Williams and Sonoma I got you."

She laughed. "No way, sweetie, you know I need a new pizza stone."

Now we were both laughing. Being with Cassandra and her family was just what I needed. The scent of cinnamon floated its way up to the second floor, forcing a giddy smile on my face. For the first time in a long time, I felt genuinely happy.

An hour later, we were all seated at the diningroom table, which was covered from end to end with food. Since I had been coming for many years, her mother knew my food-preference and had even made some of my favorite dishes, including their famous spinach dip and cauliflower gratin. I felt right at home and I absolutely adored Cassandra's parents.

"So, Amalia," Cassandra's mother said as she helped herself to a slice of ham. "How's school going? And how is that boyfriend of yours?"

Cassandra hadn't told her mother Nicholas and I had broken up. Since the whole Michael debacle, I hadn't thought about Nick too much, but I feared this conversation would ricochet me back into a sullen state.

"School's going great, Marie, but unfortunately Nicholas and I aren't together anymore." I mindlessly pushed a lump of cauliflower around my plate.

"Oh dear, I'm sorry. What happened? You two seemed so perfect for each other," Marie asked. She reached over the table and took my hand.

That had to be the worst thing someone could say, "You two seemed perfect." She was right, we were perfect, and I still couldn't give anyone a legitimate reason for him leaving me.

Before I could answer her, Cassandra chimed in. "Mom, she doesn't want to talk about it."

Cassandra's mother shook her head and then gave me an all-knowing glance. "I understand. His loss!" She patted my hand twice and then returned to her meal.

I suddenly felt the need for more wine and poured myself another rather large glass.

Dinner went by in a blur of wine and carbohydrates and before I knew it, we were having coffee and dessert. Our dessert consisted of apple pie, cupcakes with green and red food coloring, and a large vanilla cake in the shape of a snowman. Halfway through my second slice of cake, my cell phone vibrated. Not wanting to seem rude, I surreptitiously read the text message under the table.

It was from Olivia. "Hope you're having a Merry Christmas! P.S. I'm sorry for being a total bitch the other day!"

I laughed aloud and had to show the message to Cassandra. We both decided I should give Olivia another chance, and that she must have just been having an off day when she chewed me out at the restaurant. A few moments later, the phone vibrated again, and I fully expected it to be another message from Olivia. To my surprise, it was from Michael. My heart started to race as I slowly opened my inbox, savoring the moment of receiving any communication from him.

"Merry Christmas, Amalia. Hope you're having a great time at Cassandra's house."

My shoulders sank. That's all he wrote! I grimaced and passed the phone to Cassandra again.

"What's with him using your full name like that? It's very formal, like he's talking to a client or something." She rolled her eyes. "Why can't he just say Merry Christmas?"

I couldn't help but agree with her. It was the first contact we had since we hooked up the other night, and it didn't leave me feeling happy. I started coming up with all types of scenarios as to what Michael was doing at this moment and whether or not he was thinking of me, but then I remembered the promise I had made to myself to leave all of that back in the city.

After the festivities were over and the rest of the guests had left, Cassandra and I retreated to her bedroom to partake in the second part of our Christmas Eve ritual, the annual sleepover.

"I had such a blast tonight, Cass. Thank you for always letting me come here." I pulled a yellow pillowcase over her guest pillow. "I promise I'm going to come to your house for Christmas Eve for the rest of my life."

"Really? What if you marry someone who's Christian and they want to celebrate with you?" she asked, half joking, half serious.

I pretended to contemplate this dilemma and shrugged. "Well then I'll just invite him along to your house. The more the merrier, right? Or I'll spend Christmas Eve with you and Christmas Day with his family."

She cocked her head to the side and gently hit me with her pillow. "Amy, what if he wants you two to spend it with your *own* family?" she asked, raising an eyebrow for emphasis.

"You are my family." It sounded cheesy but I honestly meant every word.

"Oh shut up." She finished turning down the bed.

"So, I made this deal with myself," I said, hugging the pillow tightly. "The deal is that as long as I am in Staten Island that I wouldn't think about or talk about Michael."

"How long did you really expect that to last?"

I grabbed the blanket and wrapped it tightly around me, like a burrito. As if it was the only thing holding me together.

"It was going fine until the business-formal text message he sent me earlier," I muttered, still tightly grasping the linens. "I mean, I understand he has a girlfriend and he's probably with his family, but we are still friends, aren't we?"

"I don't know, Amalia, are you? Have the two of you even spoken about what happened?" she asked, following my lead and wrapping herself up in the blanket.

"No," I said quietly. "That's the problem, we haven't spoken about anything. Not about the kiss-attack at the hotel, not about sleeping together the other night. I don't even know how he did on the final."

"Well, what did you write back to his text message?"

"Crap, nothing!" In all of my dismay I had forgotten to even answer him.

I feverishly unwrapped myself and reached for my phone, which was currently charging on the bedside table. She reached over and took the phone out of my hands. Before I could say anything, she raised her hand in protest.

"Write something detached and non-committal," she said with a yawn, sounding like a professor of Manipulative Dating Techniques 101.

I pursed my lips and grabbed my phone out of her hand, suddenly exhausted by this conversation.

"This is ridiculous," I mumbled as I typed a message back to Michael, and tossed my phone back on the nightstand. "I wrote, *Thank you for the warm wishes, my best to you and yours*," I said. "How did that sound? Passive aggressive enough for you?"

I looked over at Cassandra but she was half asleep and no longer paying attention to my pseudo-crisis. Now I truly was determined to put all of this out of my mind. I turned on the television and lay back in bed to get ready to go to sleep. I even managed to make it through the first twenty minutes of my favorite Christmas movie, *Love Actually*, before falling asleep.

The next morning I awoke to the sweet aromas of cinnamon, toast, and fresh coffee. Followed by the all-too-loud barking of one Muffin DeLuca. The chihuahua had made her way into the bedroom and was now eagerly yapping to wake up Cassandra. I figured I would let the two of them be; this would be a perfect time to snatch my overnight bag off the dresser and grab a quick shower.

Freshly cleaned, I came downstairs to find a delicious buffet-style spread of eggs, muffins, cinnamon bagels, fresh fruit, two different types of toast, real butter (not margarine, this was a holiday after all), and freshly brewed coffee.

"Merry Christmas, Amalia. Please help yourself!" Marie smiled as she handed me a white porcelain mug.

Cassandra had already dug in, smearing a healthy amount of butter onto her perfectly toasted bagel.

"Did you sleep well, darling?" her mother asked as she poured me a rather large cup of coffee.

"I did, Marie, and thank you so much for having me over," I said, mixing half and half into my mug.

Cassandra looked up at me through tired eyes, then appeared to zone out as she redirected her attention to her coffee. Unlike me, she clearly hadn't slept well through the night. I began to wonder if Bryce had contacted her at all to wish her a Merry Christmas.

"What time are you staying until?" she asked as she poured herself another cup.

"I'm probably going to leave after breakfast. I told my parents I would spend some time with them today so they aren't too lonely on Christmas," I explained, suddenly feeling guilty for "eating and running."

"Where's your brother?" Cassandra asked. "Still at school?"

"He's actually home," I said, remembering Aaron's flight had come in yesterday morning and I had yet to contact him.

"How old is Aaron now?" Marie asked.

"He's twenty, a sophomore," was all I could say through a mouthful of berries.

Cassandra appeared to be pushing her food on her plate instead of eating it.

"What's wrong?" I whispered. "Is it Bryce? Have you heard from him?"

She shook her head no, and I thought it wise to just drop the subject.

Instead of ignoring me, she put down her utensils and motioned for me to follow her back upstairs. I politely excused myself, thanking her mother for breakfast, and followed her out of the room.

When we got upstairs, she slammed the bedroom door behind her, whipped out her laptop and opened the browser to her Facebook page. She then angrily clicked on Bryce's profile and shoved the computer in my face.

"What exactly am I looking at here?" I carefully combed through his timeline, feeling a little uneasy.

She stuck out her pointer finger and tapped on the computer screen. "Five new female friends!" she cried. "In one weekend! I mean, I know we aren't in a relationship, but the guy is screwing half of Manhattan!"

I scrolled down further and, sure enough, Bryce had acquired five new, very good-looking, very female, friends. In all honestly, this could be one of two things. One, it could be completely harmless; he went to a party or a work function and he was networking, therefore he added the women to keep in touch with them. Or two, he was a slimy Manhattan-ite douche-bag who added every girl whose name he could remember from the night before when he was out getting smashed with his buddies. From what I knew from Bryce, I expected the latter.

I closed the laptop screen and turned to face Cassandra. "Okay, what are you going to do about this?" I asked softly, trying not to anger her further. "I mean, you have been dating for about four months now and you have no control over what happens? I know what's going to happen; you're going to confront him about this and he's going to manipulate you into thinking you're crazy."

She just looked at me. At first I was expecting her to scream, to tell me I had no idea what I was talking about, and to kick me out of her house. Instead she started to sob and whispered, "I don't know if he even cares about me."

I hesitated to speak, knowing no solace I could offer would make this situation any easier. It happens all of the time in Manhattan, or anywhere for that matter. Guys string girls along for as long as they can. I wondered if in some way that was happening to me.

"Cass," I put my hand on her shoulder and gave her my best sympathetic look. "If you don't think he cares about you, then the truth is, he probably doesn't."

Again, I thought about my own situation with Michael and began to feel the same logic applied.

"I don't want to say anything because I don't want to come across as weak." She wiped her face with a tissue.

"Why would saying something to him make you seem weak?"

"Because I want to seem strong, as if none of this bothers me," she shook her head. "If he knows it bothers me then I'll seem needy, like I need validation that he's into me."

"But don't you think a strong enough person wouldn't keep quiet?" I asked as I gathered the last of my belongings. "A strong person should be able to speak up if something is bothering them, not placate the person they're with because they're afraid to say the wrong thing. I don't think you're coming off as strong." I paused before finishing my sentence, but ultimately decided she needed to hear it. "You're coming off as a pushover."

I was worried my words were too harsh and they would send Cassandra back into a tearful fit. Instead, she told me she would think about what I said, and decide if this was something she wanted to continue doing. Unfortunately, my instincts told me she wasn't going to give up on Bryce just yet.

Chapter 17

Home Sweet Home

After our discussion about Bryce – the thought of him still turned my stomach – Cassandra gave me a lift home to my parents' house.

"Hello? I'm home!" I shouted as I flung open the front door.

My parent's house was a complete contrast to Cassandra's. There was no winter wonderland, no decorations of any kind.

I expected to be greeted by my parents and brother, but no one was in sight. I knew they were home because the door was open, and we didn't live in a town where people made a habit of leaving the house with their doors unlocked.

After plopping my small suitcase down, I ran up the stairs to see what was going on. My brother was in his bedroom with his headphones on, his back to the door. I took a peek at his computer screen and saw that he was deeply engrossed in his blog. Well that explained it. I slowly crept up behind him and snatched the buds out of his ears.

"Hey! What the hell!" he said angrily until he turned around and saw I was the perpetrator. "Oh my god, Amalia!"

Aaron jumped out of his chair, nearly knocking his laptop over in the process. He grabbed me and picked me up, leaving me a little queasy, but I forgave him for it. His excitement was not unmatched; I was very happy to see my brother. Aaron and

I hadn't seen each other since he went back to school in the fall. This was the first time either of us had come home in months. Besides his animated behavior, he appeared to have just woken up, wearing a white undershirt with blue mesh basketball shorts.

"Dude, did you just get out of bed? It's almost one o'clock!" I teased, as I fluffed up his sandy blonde hair.

"Um, kind of," he answered, his cheeks turning red. "Mom and Dad went out early to go to some sort of Asian farmers' market, so I've been home alone. Can you cook something? I'm starved."

"I can make you a grilled cheese and that's about it," I said, leading the way to the kitchen. "Did Mom and Dad say what time they would be back?"

Aaron just shrugged, indicating he, in fact, probably didn't even ask them what time they were coming home. I found it a little weird that my parents had opted to leave the house so early that day when they knew I would be coming home for the first time in at least three months.

Thirty minutes and two grilled cheeses later, my parents finally returned home, arms filled with plastic shopping bags from the Asian food market. As I watched them unload the groceries onto the kitchen counter, I suddenly missed the ability to go food shopping without having to lug ten pounds of groceries back to my apartment. It's the little things in life, like being able to drive a car, that you really start to appreciate as you get older. My sudden moment of clarity was interrupted with a loud crash followed by my mother yelling at my dad to retrieve a new roll of paper towels from the closet.

"We haven't got any, Sue!" he shouted from the hallway. "I'll just grab some toilet paper."

I sat quietly at the kitchen table, absentmindedly sipping a bottle of water while this Abbot and Costello routine continued, still invisible to my parents, who had now been home an entire ten minutes. Suddenly, a roll of toilet paper came flying down the hallway, and my brother jumped in the air and caught it, like

110

an NFL superstar.

"You see what we miss when we're gone, Amalia?" Aaron said, taking an irrational amount of tissues to clean up the tiny glass cup that had broken.

"Amalia?" my mother finally said as she spun around, nearly knocking over yet another drinking glass.

I looked up from the table and gave a small wave to my parents, who were both staring at me with surprised looks on their faces.

"Hey, kiddo. What are you doing home?" my father asked, seeming flustered by my appearance.

"What are you talking about? It's Christmas Day, remember? I told you I was going to Cassandra's like I do every year on Christmas Eve, and then I was coming home the next day. Does any of this ring a bell?"

I guess it's true what they say; you really can't go home again. Or you can, and your family will look at you like a stranger when you come home for the holidays, as planned. I decided this was going to be a short visit.

"I'm sorry, sweetie, we just didn't realize it was December twenty-fifth today," my father said and he walked over to me and gave me a sympathetic hug. "You know we don't celebrate Christmas, so sometimes we lose track of these things."

"Right," I said. I glanced back over at the shopping bags on the counter, and then back to my father. "That would make sense, except you obviously knew most of the stores were closed because you went to an Asian market and not Stop and Shop."

I grew more annoyed with the lying. Instead of fighting, I shook my head and headed upstairs.

"I'm going to unpack. Don't worry, I'll be out of your hair by tomorrow."

"Amalia, wait a minute," my father called out just as I reached the second floor.

But it didn't matter, I didn't want to talk to either of them. I thought about the difference between my family and Cassandra's, how they had greeted me with open arms yesterday. It was funny how much good feelings can change in a day.

As I turned the doorknob to my bedroom, it hit me I hadn't been home since Nicholas and I broke up. I braced myself for what was undoubtedly going to be an emotional moment.

Whenever I leave home, even just for a little while, like on vacation, I always expect something to be different on my return. This, however, is never the case, even if I wish it was. My room was still exactly as I had left it, from the perfectly made bed, to the unframed Smashing Pumpkins poster, to the Dior mascara on my dresser that I had sworn was lost or possibly stolen by one of my roommates.

Still, what was once the best part of my bedroom was now the worst. Memories of Nicholas and I watching late-night movies, him taking care of me when I was sick in bed, Aaron and him arguing over whether or not the Knicks made a good trade that season; all of it came rushing back to me. Memories I didn't even know I had suddenly invaded my mind with such force I was compelled to lie down on my bed for fear if I continued standing I would surely pass out. I looked to the right of my bed, and there proudly displayed on my bedside table was a photo of us taken on our vacation to Cape Cod merely six months ago. I picked up the frame and studied the picture. I was wearing a long white flowing sundress with bright-coral sandals that I had bought specifically for our summer vacation. I had a deep tan, very rare for my pale complexion, and my curls were platinum from being in the sun. It seemed like a lifetime ago. I thought about how perfect everything felt, lying on the beach, talking about our future together and joking about asking the hotel manager if we could get married right there and then. How did things get so messed up? If Nicholas had these same memories that I did, how could he have just let everything go? I took the picture of us out of the frame, studied it one more time, and then ripped it up into tiny pieces until it was impossible to rip them anymore.

I stood up and started to unpack a few things; I was only going to stay here the night but I didn't want to live out of the suitcase, at least not in my own house.

"Knock, knock," Aaron said as he made his way into my now-messy bedroom.

"How goes it, little brother?" I asked with a small smile. It was all I could muster up at the moment. "Tell me about Syracuse." My brother was now a junior at the state university of Syracuse, and I honestly still couldn't believe how old he had gotten. He sat down next to me and took the shirt I was folding out of my hand.

"Forget school," he said. "What's going on with you? You seem, I don't know, a little lost."

He nailed it; that's exactly what I was, lost.

"Well, Nicholas and I broke up," I offered.

"I know," he said. "Facebook told me."

"Oh good, that site did my dirty work for me," I said sarcastically.

"So, have you been seeing someone new?"

Even though Aaron was twenty years old, a grown-up for all intents and purposes, I still pictured him as my baby brother, and would probably always have trouble talking to him about relationships. Regardless, I honestly didn't know how to answer the question presented to me.

"It's complicated," I said retrieving my shirt from his hands.

"Well, sis, whoever this guy is, you make sure he treats you right." He made his way to the door. "If he doesn't, you tell him your brother's gonna come to the big city and kick his ass. Okay?"

I rolled my eyes. "You can shut the door behind you."

A few minutes later, unpacked and room cleared of Nicholas mementos, I found myself wondering what Michael was up to. I reached for the cell phone and then hesitated. What was I afraid of? Weren't we still friends? Just a quick hello, I decided. My heart pounded harder with each letter I typed into my phone, until I finally hit send. I took a deep breath and glanced in the mirror. I could always feel the physical effect Michael had on me, but

113

this was the first time I had seen it. My face was beet-red and my pupils were dilated to the point where I just looked like I had just had an eye exam. I felt a wave of embarrassment roll over me as I realized this was how I must look to him all the time. A red-faced, black-eyed lunatic.

A few minutes later he wrote back, asking me when I was coming back home. I was glad he answered so quickly. It always got to me how some people could go an hour without answering you. I went to type that I was home, and then remembered he was probably referring to Manhattan.

I wrote, "Coming back soon, maybe tomorrow. I've been home for one day and it's already too much."

A few more minutes went by; no response. Maybe he *was* the type to wait an hour to respond. I decided I would go for a run and clear my head. Also, it was a good excuse to get out of the house while still enjoying my neighborhood. I used to run all of the time, but since I had moved to my apartment, the interest had gotten away from me. I suddenly felt like a make-up run. I had to dress warmly, since it was the end of December and thirty degrees outside. I threw on leggings with yoga pants over them, a sports bra, a tank top, a long-sleeved shirt, and an Under Armor sweatshirt over the entire ensemble. I grabbed my iPod out of my purse, slipped on my sneakers and bolted outside.

The run wasn't too bad; sure, it was freezing, but after the first half mile I had worked up enough energy to keep warm. I ran a full three miles before feeling a cramp in my side and deciding to call it a day.

When I got back to my house, everyone was gone. Thank God, I thought as I made my way into a much-needed shower. The shower felt so great after my run, I knew I would be extremely sore tomorrow but I didn't care. I needed that time to myself to let out some stress.

After my shower I was so relaxed I had forgotten all about texting Michael. That was until I saw my activity light blinking on the top of my phone. Sure enough, he had written back, even if his reply was an hour after the fact.

"I'm coming back to the city tomorrow," he wrote, followed by another message that read, "If you are around tomorrow afternoon, we should get together."

Before my brain could come up with an excuse as to why this was a bad idea, I wrote, "Yep, I will be there. See you tomorrow," and hit send.

Just the thought of getting to see Michael tomorrow was enough to send me into full anxiety mode. My heart began beating a mile a minute and a herd of butterflies rummaged through my stomach. I plopped back down on my bed and tried to compose myself, avoiding all mirrors this time. I let out a soft chuckle. So much for my relaxing run.

Chapter 18

Words between words

Completely normal, non-anxious, well-adjusted people have that virtue called patience. I am not one of them. So when Michael asked me to meet him for lunch at a quaint uptown restaurant, of which I had already forgotten the name, and was now running fifteen minutes late, I began to essentially freak out. Most people, who are not me, would sit down and order a drink, maybe check their email or Facebook, and be fine while waiting for the rest of their party to arrive. I, however, had already checked my phone twice, text messaging myself to make sure the damn thing was working, and had run at least six different possible scenarios in my head as to why Michael was going to stand me up, including one very graphic daydream where his girlfriend had found out about us and has already murdered him with a Waterford cake knife from Bergdorf's, and was coming for me next.

I decided to order a glass of white wine to take the edge off when finally Michael made his way through the door. He darted toward me, briefcase in hand, and took the seat across from me.

"Hey. I'm so sorry I'm late. Fifth Avenue is a wreck. I was sitting in traffic for almost half an hour!" He flung his coat over the back of the chair.

"It's not a problem," I said as casually as I could. "It took you that long to get here from your apartment?"

"No I just came from a meeting across town," he said taking a long gulp of water.

I felt stunted for conversation and a slight awkward silence opened up, which I felt compelled to fill. "I ordered a glass of wine while I was waiting, but it still hasn't come yet."

Riveting conversation, I thought, as I pulled the menu up to bury my face. How could someone have such a strong effect on me? I've slept with other guys; hell I've been in love with other guys, but no one has ever had such a unique paralyzing effect over me. After we made plans last night to meet this afternoon, I fell asleep early and dreamt mostly about this encounter all night. It's always strange to see someone the day after you've dreamt about them. I wonder if he knew; if he could sense it.

A few moments later, the waiter came with my wine and Michael took the opportunity to order a scotch.

"Mushroom ravioli?" Michael asked.

"Excuse me?"

He offered me a wry smile. "That's what you're going to order, I know you. Plus, it sounds delicious."

I rolled my eyes in an attempt to cover up how happy I was that he remembered I was a huge fan of mushrooms.

"You think you know me so well, eh?" I folded the menu and placed it on the edge of the table.

Michael just grinned and my heart skipped a simultaneous beat. I had been on countless dates with men who would try to get me to chow down on a medium-rare burger. It was refreshing to be with someone who paid attention to my preferences.

"How was Christmas? Did you go to Cassandra's?" Michael asked slowly, sipping his scotch.

"Christmas Eve was great," I said, recalling the wonderful meal at the DeLuca residence. "Christmas Day, on the other hand, was another story." I offered him an eye roll.

"What do you mean?" he asked, leaning closer to me.

"Well, in true Hastings fashion, my parents accidentally forgot I was coming home," I said, swirling my wine around. "I did get to spend time with my brother, which was great because I barely see him, but other than that I couldn't wait to come back to the city."

"What do you mean forgot? How could your parents have forgotten you were coming home?" Michael asked sympathetically.

"Well, we've never exactly been close. Sometimes I feel like an outsider looking in on my own family, like a stranger. When I see how they interact with Aaron, I get more upset than I'd like. It's as if the three of them are a family without me."

Michael probably didn't want to hear about this and I immediately asked him how his Christmas was in an attempt to change the subject. Before he could answer, I heard a voice behind me.

"Ravioli?"

"What? Oh yeah. That's mine," I turned to the waitress, who looked more like she was working at a night club than a restaurant.

He didn't seem to notice her. He kept his eyes on me until she left.

"My Christmas was fine," he said, digging into his grilled chicken. "I saw my family, nothing special."

Twenty minutes later Michael motioned for the check and paid the entire bill before I could even offer an obligatory reach for my wallet. A sudden wave of sadness swamped me; lunch was over and I now had to trek all the way back downtown, alone.

"I live about ten blocks from here if you want to come by," Michael said as we walked out of the restaurant.

Before I could give him a chance to change his mind, I said yes and we hailed a cab down to 60th Street. When we pulled up in front of Michael's apartment building, it suddenly dawned on me that I had never seen where he lived before. The apartment building looked brand new, clearly less than five years old, and extremely swanky. The doorman greeted us upon arrival, referring to Michael as "Mr. Rathbourne," and then held the elevator door open for us. I felt like royalty as we rode up to the thirtieth floor. The apartment was as gorgeous as I imagined, illuminated by large elongated windows reaching from the ceiling down to the floor. Even though it was only one bedroom, his home was very spacious, including a large living room, a reasonably sized kitchen, a bedroom and two bathrooms. Like mine, his kitchen counters were covered in new sparkling granite, which looked even better when contrasted with a matte, off-white backsplash and rich hardwood floors. A jet-black refrigerator and ceiling-suspended pots and pans pulled the entire room together. Just to the left was the living room, cleverly decorated with reprinted classic art, sandalwood-scented reed diffusers, and a self-made bookshelf, filled from top to bottom, that covered nearly an entire wall of the room. The whole apartment was a vision, something out of *House and Garden*, pristinely clean, and I could not believe that a twenty-three-year-old man lived here. I was beginning to wonder if Michael had a trust fund.

He took my coat and led me to the couch, where we had a two-hour-long conversation about school, our friends, and how glad we were to have a few weeks off from doing work.

I checked the time and noticed it was getting late and already pitch black outside. That's the thing about winter in New York; just when you start to get your day going 5:00 hits, and the sun is gone. I decided I should leave and head home before the weather became too unbearably cold. I stood up to gather my things, but before I could so much as put my shoes on, Michael grabbed my arm again, the way he had the night of the NYU dinner, and pulled me toward him. We started kissing passionately, all inhibitions out the window. Michael lifted me up and pushed me into the wall. I pulled hard at his clothes, silently begging for him to take them off. The next thing I knew, I was being carried past the living room, into the bedroom, and being plopped onto the bed.

The next morning I awoke to piercing sunlight coming through the window and dancing on my face. Through tired eyes, I reached for the bottle of water I usually kept on my nightstand, but to my dismay found nothing. That's when I realized I was not in my own bed. For a brief moment I began to panic and wondered where I was and how I got here, retracing my steps from the night before. I slowly turned around to find Michael lying right next to me, still sound asleep, with his arms carefully cradled around me.

Some people look like disasters in the morning, with unimaginable bed head and crusty eyes, not to mention morning breath. However, none of those unfavorable characteristics were present here this morning. At least, not with him. I had no access to a mirror and had no idea what I would be dealing with when I finally collected all my energy and made my way to a bathroom. Michael's brown hair had fallen into a perfect sexy-messy look this morning, while he sported the exact right amount of facial scruff. Suddenly self-conscious about my own appearance, I gently untangled myself from his grasp, and crawled to the edge of the bed. Before my first foot could hit the floor, I was boomeranged back into his arms and gently locked under the blanket.

"Good morning," he mumbled dreamily, still holding onto me tightly.

"Good morning to you too," I said, all too happy to be back in his arms.

"You don't want to get up just yet, Amalia," he said. "It's way too cold out and the bed is so inviting and warm."

He did have a point; I wasn't exactly in any rush to go home. I reached for my phone and saw that I had two missed calls from Cassandra; one from last night and one from ten minutes ago. I sent her a quick text saying I'd call her later, and put my phone back on the nightstand.

Michael and I lay in bed half asleep for another forty-five minutes, until he finally suggested a cup of coffee. Against my will, I exited the bed and stumbled into the bathroom to get dressed. I had no recollection of putting on his Cornell alumni T-shirt to sleep in, but with a hint of sadness I peeled it off and returned to the outfit I had on last night. A glimpse in the mirror revealed dark smudged make-up that actually didn't look all that bad. The brown eye shadow had run on into the crease of my eyes, creating a smoldering effect. I reached into my purse and grabbed a light-pink lipstick. I ran the tube across my mouth and then dotted some of the make-up onto my cheekbones to give my face some much-needed color. I ran my fingers through my hair in an attempt to tame the blonde bird's nest and took a step back to make sure I was decent enough to go back into the living room. When I emerged from the bathroom, I was shocked to find that not only was the coffee brewed and prepared, but Michael stood at the stove preparing fried cheese omelets, complete with freshly chopped tomatoes and parsley, and what appeared to be whole-grain toast to accompany it. I slowly crossed to him, and he just smiled and handed me a cup of coffee.

"Milk and two sugars, for you," he smiled. "Sorry I didn't have the ingredients for a soy latte, but I hope this will suffice."

"It's perfect," I said as I took a seat at the small table in the corner of the kitchen. "It's all perfect. Thank you for making this."

We ate our breakfast in a comfortable silence and I thought about how happy I felt. My happiness was quickly interrupted by the harsh reminder that Michael was not mine, he belonged to Marge. I was renting him, well actually, more of an illegal sublet kind of situation. I thought about bringing it up, about asking him if he and Marge were still dating and if so, was he going to break up with her? Even through all of this confusion, I believed he had feelings for me. Why else would he go through all of the trouble of helping me with school? Or cooking me breakfast in the morning? If I was merely a booty call, he would have made up an excuse about an early meeting and politely asked me to leave. Instead here we were, eating eggs and drinking coffee. I decided, as wonderful as this was, I wouldn't give him the opportunity to kick me out. I finished the last of my coffee and got up to clear my dishes off the table.

"Stop," he said, as he wiped his face with a napkin. "I got this."

He stood and cleared both of our plates and immediately loaded them into the dishwasher.

"Thank you for everything, but I really should be going," I said as I grabbed my coat off the edge of the couch.

After our perfect evening together, I expected him to put up a small fight, to insist we spend the day together, or at least a long drawn-out kiss goodbye. Instead, "I'll talk to you soon," was all he said. He walked me to the door and gave me a hug.

Disappointed that I didn't even get a kiss goodbye, I made my way outside into the freezing December air, and walked to the subway station alone.

Chapter 19

Resolutions

"I'm freezing!" Cassandra cried as we made our way to Libation, a chic club on the Lower East Side, that night.

New Year's Eve was a fresh start as far as I was concerned, and tonight we were going to party it up. I glanced over at Cassandra, taking note of her outfit. Of course she was freezing. She was wearing a paper-thin coat with a sleeveless silver dress underneath, no stockings and strappy black sandals.

We finally turned on to Ludlow Street and I shouted, "We're here!"

We had decided to walk to the bar after dinner instead of taking a cab in a concerted effort to save money, since we'd be blowing a large wad of dough this evening. I checked my watch as we walked past a crowd of rowdy teenagers. Ten forty-five; plenty of time before the ball dropped.

The line to get into the bar was literally around the corner. A deep shudder shook me as I realized we were nowhere near getting out of the cold. Without hesitation, Cassandra made a beeline for the bouncer, who held one hand up to stop her from walking any further.

"Cassandra DeLuca," she stated proudly as she began to unbutton her long Armani coat. "We're on the list."

And sure enough, we were. She practically handed the bouncer her coat, before he motioned to the coat check inside. I should have known better than to assume we'd be waiting on line like the rest of New York; one call from Cassie's boss and we were VIPs anywhere in the city.

The inside of the club was beautifully decorated with an elegant winter theme. Sparkling snowflakes and silver Christmas lights lined the wooden bar. I felt a chill run through me; the kind that happens when you feel excited and can't quite place why.

"What do you want?" Cassandra asked, pointing to the bar.

"Champagne!" I said with a smile. "I'm feeling festive."

I felt a hand on my shoulder and quickly turned around to see who it was. In true creepy fashion, Alex had snuck up behind me and was now greeting me with a smirk.

"Good tidings to you, Miss Hastings," he said as he took a swig of what was most likely a glass of scotch. "I was hoping you would be here."

"How did you get past the line?" I asked, suddenly feeling less elite from being on the list.

"I'm friends with the bartender."

Unwilling to further engage in this conversation, I asked him if he had seen Olivia and Michael yet.

"Yes, Olivia just arrived a moment before you, but I'm afraid our dear Michael isn't coming this evening," he said with a smirk, or maybe I was imagining things.

Pain stabbed my chest as I heard these words. I was under the impression our entire group would be here tonight and sudden anger rose up inside me when I realized that Michael wouldn't be joining us. Albeit unfounded anger, but anger nonetheless.

"What do you mean he isn't coming? I thought we all agreed to spend New Year's together?" I uttered, trying not to sound as desperately defeated and betrayed as I felt.

"I don't know. He told me he got a last-minute flight to Phoenix to spend tonight with his girlfriend."

I could barely process the information. Michael wasn't here because he was in Phoenix with his girlfriend? My anger suddenly turned to sadness and then to guilt.

"Oh, I didn't know they were still together," I said softly, tears warming up behind my eyes.

Just then Olivia swooped in and wrapped her arms around me.

"Amalia! I'm so happy to see you, Happy New Year! Listen, I am really sorry for being world-class bitch to you the other day, it was completely unwarranted," she said apologetically.

I shook my head to tell her everything was all right, but also in an attempt to collect myself.

"Olivia, please. It happened last year already!" I said trying my best at the obvious joke.

"Yes, good one," she said giving me a light punch on the arm. "Where's Michael tonight?"

Alex was making his way toward the men's room and I figured it was safe to talk.

"He's in Phoenix," I said feeling the tears build up again and felt worried that they would stream down my face in the most obvious way. "He's with Marge."

Olivia took a step back and looked as if she was contemplating this information. "It's so weird, he doesn't even talk about her. If we never asked him if he was single back in the beginning of the year, I bet he never would have even told us about her. I mean he's one of our best friends, and he didn't even tell us he was going to Arizona or anything."

I just shook my head, unable to form words. Of course I had thought about this many times. I had even once thought "Marge" wasn't real, just a ploy Michael used to stay single so he could focus on his schoolwork without the distractions of dating. It was becoming irrevocably clear that Marge was real, was Michael's girlfriend, and that I was in fact the other woman.

Cassandra returned, champagne in hand, and asked what we were talking about. I gave her a quick synopsis of the last five minutes' conversation, and downed my champagne in two gulps.

"Holy crap," she said taking a long gulp of her own drink. "Good thing tonight's an open bar."

Just then Alex reemerged with someone. As they drew closer, I realized it was Bryce. Cassandra had "accidentally" forgotten to mention he would be joining us tonight, and she gave me a sheepish look as she sipped her bubbly. Bryce crossed to Cassandra and gave her a kiss on the forehead.

"Hey, Amalia, how have you been?" He flashed me an over-the-top smile. I wondered if he was high, or already drunk from before.

"I'm great!" I said matching his faux enthusiasm. "Everybody ready to ring in the New Year together? Well not everybody, exactly, one of us is missing." Great, now I was the one who had too much to drink.

"Who's missing?" Bryce said to Cassandra.

"Excuse me," I said placing my champagne flute on the nearest table.

I walked out of the main room of the bar and stumbled into what I hoped was the ladies' room. I burst through the stall, feverishly locked the door, and began to cry. Someone knocked softly on the door of the stall and said, "Amalia." I opened the door to see Olivia standing there with pity all over her face.

"I'm fine," I pushed past her to get to the sink. I caught a glimpse of myself in the mirror. My professionally done, smoky eye make-up was now smeared all over my face. I looked like a battered wife. I started to clean up with a wet napkin, but quickly gave up. "I'm going home. I don't want to be here anymore. I can't watch Cassandra and Bryce kiss at midnight, I can't listen to Alex say another sardonic sentence, and I can't keep wishing Michael was here with me instead of in Phoenix with her."

I sounded so pathetic, my own voice was irritating me and everyone in this bathroom must think I was either crazy or on drugs.

"Okay, then we'll leave," Olivia shrugged.

Without another word, she grabbed my clutch off the sink and held my hand through the crowded dance floor as we made our way to the exit.

When we got outside, Olivia hailed a cab and I sent Cassie a quick text telling her what happened, and that I'd talk to her tomorrow.

"Where ya goin?" the cabbie said with a thick Brooklyn accent.

I was too upset to speak. Olivia gave him my address and ten minutes later, we were outside my apartment. To my surprise, Olivia got out of the cab with me. "I'm coming up."

"No, I'm fine. Go back to the party," I pleaded, now feeling horribly guilty for allowing her to leave with me.

She cocked her head to the side and made her way into my building.

"You're not going up there!" I said.

She just shook her head and said, "Oh, but I am."

The next thing I knew it was 11:55, and Olivia and I were on my couch in pajamas, sharing a gallon of cookie-dough ice-cream, and watching "Dick Clark's Rockin' New Year's Eve."

"He's a jerk," she said, spooning a large bite into her mouth.

"It's my own fault; I'm an idiot," I said as I followed suit with my own spoonful of creamy goodness. Who knew ice cream and red wine made such a delicious combination?

"What's your resolution?" Olivia said to me while still staring at the television.

I had to think about this one. I never had a resolution before, but this year it seemed important, almost necessary. This was the year I lost my true love, the year I started to seriously question my intelligence because of how badly I was doing in graduate school, and the year one of my best friends willingly made me his mistress.

I turned to Olivia, who was now silently mouthing the countdown. "To be stronger."

She turned to me and smiled approvingly, as Ryan Seacrest

129

said, "Three, Two, One. Happy New Year!"

Chapter 20

Back to normal

"It's a good thing we registered for this class early," Olivia said to me as she pulled her laptop out of a hideous over-sized computer bag. "It's packed!"

She was right. Today was January eleventh, and we were back at school for our second semester. Since this class was a core requirement, Michael and Alex would also undoubtedly be on the roster. I hadn't seen Michael since our bed-and-breakfast date at his apartment over two weeks ago. I received one text message from him yesterday morning asking if I was ready for classes to begin again. I left it unanswered.

"Good morning, class. This is Intro to Cognitive Psychology, and my name is Dr. Adrienne Bakowski, and this class will be held on Monday mornings from 10 a.m. until 1 p.m.," said a middle-aged, stocky woman with mousy brown hair and thick round glasses.

She dropped a stack of textbooks on her desk and continued her introduction.

"If you are running late to this class, turn yourself around and go back home. I won't have anyone walking into my classroom fifteen minutes late and disrupting my lecture. Any questions?" she barked.

The room fell silent. We all looked around at each other like our boat was about to sink and it was time to start deciding who gets the life vests. I opened my notebook and knocked my pen off the desk and watched horrified as it rolled down the atrium stairs. Thankfully, Bakowski didn't seem to notice; unfortunately it was my only pen. For a moment I honestly considered quitting – just standing up and walking out in a Jerry McGuire-inspired "Who's coming with me?" fashion. Instead, I took a deep breath and reminded myself that in four short months, school would be over and I would be in Brazil.

I didn't take a single note that day. Instead I sat in class and thought long and hard about telling Michael I couldn't see him anymore. I practiced a monologue in my head and imagined different outcomes of the scenario. I quickly realized not seeing each other was impossible, and that we not only went to school together but had the same group of friends, and would inevitably be working together in the somewhat near future. At exactly one o'clock on the dot, Dr. Bakowski dismissed us, and a chorus of relieved sighs filled the classroom.

"Well that was brutal," Olivia said to me as she packed up her belongings. "I am in serious need of a caffeine fix, you in?"

Before I answered, I skimmed the room and found Alex chatting to Michael. On cue, my heart started to pound. The two seemed to be in a deep discussion, probably discussing in great detail today's lecture, only furthering my guilt about not taking any notes.

"Yes, absolutely. Let's get out of here," I said with urgency partly because I could really use a cup of coffee, but mostly because I didn't want to run into Michael.

Chapter 21

A concerted effort

I was proud of myself. Two weeks had gone by and I had done my best to put any thoughts of Michael or Nick out of my mind and concern myself mainly with my schoolwork. I was hitting NYU's Bobst Library almost every night, and even managed to talk one of my professors into letting me do a small extra credit assignment, to guarantee a higher grade in the class. The next step in my valiant effort to detox from all things men was to find a paying internship in the city. Although my parents had agreed to support me while I was in graduate school, I still felt like I was taking charity and that spending their money somehow gave them power over me. Not to mention the added work would get me out of the apartment, in which, besides the library, I had been spending nearly every waking moment. The words "shut-in" had escaped Cassandra's lips earlier that day when she asked me to meet her for lunch. I declined the offer, saying I had to polish the hardwood floors and make sure my closet was coordinated in accordance to fabric weight.

By two o'clock on this Tuesday afternoon I had already done my laundry, taken a long bubble bath, dusted every inch of exposed space in my bedroom, and unloaded the dishwasher. I didn't have class today so I prepared myself for my next adventure, which was to tackle the grime in the bathroom which had no doubt taken over the bathtub. I was just about to put on my oversized latex gloves when I heard the door open.

"Christina?" I called out, but heard no response.

I figured she had her headphones on and proceeded to the bathroom, where I was greeted by no less than an hour's worth of mildew. As I began to spray the sticky tub with Fantastic, I heard the unmistakable clacking of high heels on the hardwood floor and knew it was not Christina arriving home. I dropped the cleaning products and spun around to find Cassandra once again standing in my doorway with her hands on her hips.

"Breaking and entering now?" I asked, as I snapped off my gloves and walked out of the bathroom.

She followed me into the living room and we both plopped down on the sofa.

"No, I am not breaking into your home," she said with an exasperated sigh. "Your neighbor was leaving, so I asked him to hold the door for me because I had forgotten my key."

I unscrewed the cap of my much-needed water bottle. "You don't have a key. You do realize you don't actually live here, right?"

"Very funny, Amalia. Had you left the apartment in the past two weeks, I wouldn't have had to take such drastic measures to see you." She kicked off her Louboutins.

I knew she made a good amount of money, but I was always stunned when I saw her wearing seven-hundred-dollar shoes.

"I've left the apartment—" I started to say, but she quickly put her hand up and cut me off.

"Leaving the apartment to go to your boring class and to the boring library does not a social life make." She stole my water bottle and took a large gulp. "Now I am giving you exactly one hour to get your shit together and come with me to Alfangi Salon, where you will be getting a haircut because, let's face it, you need one. Followed by an early dinner at Morandi, and then we are meeting Bryce and his friend Hayden for drinks at The Rusty Knot."

Everything she said sounded wonderful enough, well maybe except the part about spending the evening with Bryce and his no doubt pretentious friend, but I still had my reservations about emerging back into the social scene. Since it was the first time people would be seeing me out in a while, I thought I should still make an effort to look good.

Before I could answer, Cassandra tossed the water bottle onto the couch and clicked on the television. "Go get dressed, I'll wait here."

Exactly one hour later, I re-emerged as a fully-dressed, fully made-up, somewhat put together woman. Cassandra dropped the back issue of Elle she was reading and stood.

"Well it's nice to see you can still dress yourself." She brushed a piece of lint off my black knit top. "Now let's see what we can do about that hair."

I once read that January is the coldest month in New York, but I have to disagree and protest that February has it beat. The twenty-degree wind slapped me in the face as we hailed our cab up to midtown, and I quickly regretted allowing Cassandra talk me into leaving the house.

When we finally got to the salon, I was bombarded with over-friendly, and overly thin, employees who quickly offered me everything from a bone-dry cappuccino, to what I was pretty sure was an offer of Quaaludes. I settled for the coffee and sat idly by as Cassie brought over an obviously gay hair stylist. He was wearing a bright-green pashmina, dark-gray skinny jeans, an ironic T-shirt that cleverly said "A cut above the rest," and vintage beige Chuck Taylor sneakers to pull it all together. They chattered in Italian and ran their fingers through my hair like I was their My Size Barbie.

"Now, Amalia," Cassandra started as she put both hands on my shoulders and leaned over me. "You are in very good hands. My dear friend Anthony is going to take very good care of you, isn't that right, Anthony?"

I looked up at the pashmina-clad gentleman, expecting him to comfort me into trusting him with my hair, but all he said was, "*Si*," and then grabbed a pair of scissors out of the top drawer. Cassandra gave me a small pat on the head, and then turned toward the exit.

"Hey, Cassandra, you told them I just wanted a trim, right?" I called out as Cassie was halfway out the door.

"Amalia, you have to stop worrying so much!" she said. "Now I have an important phone call to make to Gwyneth's people. I'll be back in forty-five minutes. You should be just about finished by then."

Before I could open my mouth to say another word, the door closed and I was alone with Anthony the hair stylist.

Twenty minutes passed and I was starting to get nervous about the outcome of my hair. Anthony had turned me away from the mirror after my second attempt at sneaking a peak. As I flipped through an old magazine, my phone vibrated in my pocket. It was an email from an address I didn't recognize. I decided to open it anyway because the sender had opted to use my professional email address, and it might be the human resources department from one of the hospitals I had applied to intern at. I nearly fell off my chair when I it was not in fact someone emailing to offer me a job. It was Nicholas's sister Marissa. I almost forgot where I was and started to get out of my chair when Anthony pushed me back into the seat and shook his finger angrily at me. I took a deep breath and began to read the email.

Amalia,

Hope all is well with you! I am writing to you because I remember you asking when our store was going to have another Friends and Family sale and we are actually having one this weekend.

Hope to see you there!

-M

My whole body ignited with rage. I hadn't heard from Nicholas or any of his friends or family members in three months, and his sister was emailing me to tell me about some bullshit sale her boutique was having!

I quickly ordered myself to calm down, thinking back to a few breathing exercises I learned from yoga. Nicholas had been out of my life for months, but the mere reminder of his existence could ruin my entire day. I still missed him more than I let on. The only thing that distracted me from the pain of missing him was the pain from dealing with Michael. For a moment I considered what to write back. If I sounded angry, it would come off as petty and surely would get back to Nicholas. I decided to take the high road and come off as aloof as possible. I opened a blank email and began to type.

Marissa,
All is well, thanks for asking! Thank you for the invitation. Can't this weekend but maybe next time.
-A

I smiled to myself and hit send.

Just then, Anthony spun me around in the chair. He snapped the black robe off my neck and said, *"Fin."*

After a deep breath, I took a look in the mirror. My hair was at least two inches shorter with deep short layers in the back and a long side bang over my right eye. I let out a heavy sigh and got up to examine myself closer in the mirror. I had to admit, the guy knew what he was doing. My hair never looked so good. The length made me look professional but still young, and the angles around my face made my eyes look huge. I reached into my wallet and tipped him a healthy twenty-five percent and thanked him profusely.

The sound of high heels filled the room, and I turned around to see Cassandra making her way toward me.

"Well?" she said as she slowly pulled off her oversized sunglasses.

"Well, you tell me. What do you think?" I did a dramatic twirl and finished it off with a superfluous hair flip.

She folded her arms in her signature way and said with a wide grin, "I think we're ready to meet the boys for drinks later."

A few hours later, we were finished with dinner at Morandi and were making our way to The Rusty Knot to meet Bryce and his friend for drinks.

"So wait, what's this guy's name again? You know, Bryce's friend." I took a sip of my Jack and Coke.

"His name is Hayden and he works for Merrill Lynch as a financial advisor," she said.

"Oh, so another yuppie," I said with a smirk.

"You should keep your options open, missy," she wagged her finger and she stole a sip of my drink. "You're a single woman, a free agent. Don't just write someone off like that."

I looked at her and tilted my head. "Wow, Cass, that was actually really profound and insightful. I almost feel inspired."

"Yeah, I know," she said and took a shot of tequila. "Plus, he's totally hot and rich."

"Right, of course." I laughed.

"While we're on the topic of men, have you heard from Michael at all?"

The mere mention of Michael's name made me feel weak like a child. "No. No Michael." I was going to need another drink. "But I did receive an email from Nicholas's sister while I was in the salon."

"What!" She started to say more, but I pointed to Bryce who had just walked into the bar and motioned for her to be quiet.

The last thing I needed was Bryce's input in my life. Walking directly behind him was a tall, well-dressed man who I assumed must be Hayden.

"Hey, babe," Bryce said giving Cassandra a quick peck.

She stood up from the barstool and immediately went in for a long hug. Annoyance pinged at how eager Cassie was to see Bryce.

I realized I was being rude and turned to Hayden and gave him a small smile.

"Hi, Amalia, I'm Hayden." He extended his hand to greet me.

"Nice to meet you, Hayden." I accepted his light handshake.

He gave me a big smile, while holding onto my hand for a few seconds. His eye contact was strong, and his dark-green eyes were wide and youthful, which was a strong juxtaposition to the rest of his features, which were classic and masculine. An attraction immediately drew me, followed by a strong rush of annoyance. I didn't need to feel attracted to anyone else right now, certainly not one of Bryce's undoubtedly douche-bag friends. I pulled my hand away and suggested we get a table since the bar stools were quickly filling up.

"So, Amalia, do you have a new boyfriend yet?" Bryce said as he leaned over the table and passed me my drink.

"Nope, not yet, Bryce," I said putting my annoyance in my tone. "I'm trying to work on myself right now."

I reached for my wallet to pay him back for my drink, but he waved me away. Bryce and Cassandra had chosen to sit next to each other in the booth, so I was pressed up against Hayden. I was close enough to smell his cologne, or maybe it was his aftershave.

"Miss Amalia is going to Brazil this summer," Bryce said.

"Oh really?" Hayden turned to me, seeming genuinely interested. "That's amazing, I bet you'll have a wonderful experience."

"Yeah, I really can't wait to go," I uttered, wondering if that was still true.

"I'll be stuck here in the city all summer," said Cassandra, teasingly.

"There are worse places to be stuck," said Bryce. "Like, anywhere else for example."

"What do you mean?" Cassandra asked.

"I mean, I love it here. There's so much to do at any given point in the day," he offered.

"Sure," I nodded, having to agree with him on that. "But don't you feel like the city gets a little redundant after a while?"

"Redundant?" he asked, with an air of arrogance. "No, of course not."

I should bow out of this conversation, before starting a fight with Cassie's new love interest.

"I don't want to live here my whole life," Cassandra said. "This country is huge and I've always been a New Yorker. To me, living in another city or even a rural area seems exotic."

"That's ridiculous," Bryce said, snickering. "If you moved somewhere else, you'd be incredibly bored after only a few months. I'm never moving out of Manhattan."

This sentence shocked me. Sure, I loved Manhattan as much as the next twenty-three-year-old did, but the idea of being here my entire life seemed limiting.

"What exactly would I miss so much?" Cassandra challenged. "Hopefully in a few years I'll be successful enough to be able to work from anywhere, or maybe I'll change fields altogether."

"You'd miss a lot, Cass," he said, seeming irritated for having to defend New York City. "For one, you'd miss the nightlife. You'd definitely miss all of the restaurants and bars, and you'd really just miss all of the culture."

"The culture?" I chimed in, crossing my arms.

"Yes, Amalia," Bryce snapped. "The culture."

"Staying in one place your entire life doesn't make you cultured," Cassandra said. "You're shutting yourself off to real culture. Sure, Manhattan makes it easy for you. You have lots of different people living here, conveniently giving you little tastes of different lifestyles. But if you want to see real culture, you're eventually going to have to leave the island, babe."

Bryce looked stunned. This was the first time I'd ever seen Cassie talk back to him; evidently, it was the first time.

"So, Amalia," Hayden said, desperate to change the subject. "Traveling aside, why are you single?"

"That's such a hard question to answer!" I said, laughing. "I don't have some major plan in mind, I'm just taking a little time to work on myself, I guess."

"Don't spend too long working on yourself," Hayden said, offering me a weak smile.

I shook my head, caught off guard by this statement.

"What do you mean by that?" I asked, genuinely interested.

"You don't want to spend too much time focusing on being alone, because if you meet a great person, you'll end up passing them up." He looked around the table.

I had the feeling this statement wasn't only directed toward me. Maybe it was a cleverly hidden dig at Bryce, who had been dating Cassandra for about five months now with no sign of committing.

"He has a point," Cassandra said as she swiped on a fresh coat of lip-gloss.

She and Bryce had moved on from their spat and were holding hands.

"Well, Hayden, do you have a girlfriend?" I asked.

Before he could answer, Bryce chimed in. "Nope, he is as single as they come!"

Bryce and Cassandra sat in the booth and stared at me with fake creepy smiles, and I realized it was official. I was being set up.

An hour later, Cassandra and Bryce made up some excuse about having to get up early and left Hayden and me alone at the bar for one more round.

"So what did Bryce mean when he said you're as single as can be?" I asked.

Hayden and I were now at opposite ends of the booth, making our conversation less uncomfortable. He leaned back in his seat and contemplated this question.

Finally he said, "I'm tired of the games, you know? I'm at the point in my life where I want to settle down. I'm done with the dating scene and the work-obsessed girls I seem to attract. I guess what I'm saying is, I'm ready for *the one*."

I let out a heavy sigh. The last man I heard talk this way was

143

Nicholas.

"I used to feel that way," I started and then realized I needed to take a break because I hadn't spoken about Nicholas in a long time. "I was with someone who I believed to be my soul-mate."

Hayden put his drink down and leaned over the table toward me.

"What happened?" he said with what seemed to be genuine concern.

"He left me, and now I'm broken," I said, feeling the tears well up from behind my eyes. It was a pretty dramatic statement, but it was still how I felt.

Hayden reached over and put both of his hands on top of mine. I quickly pulled them away and wiped the tears away from my eyes.

"I know you feel that way now, but you won't always. And it's completely his loss. You should never have to spend all of your time chasing someone, even if it's just the idea of someone. Or the idea of how they were. I truly meant what I said before," he said as he motioned toward the server for the bill. "Don't close yourself off from something that could be good because you get too lost in focusing on other things. You might not want it right now, but you don't want to wake up a few months from now and realize you gave up a good thing."

I couldn't say anything. I was afraid if I opened my mouth to speak, I would cry.

As I walked home, I thought about what Hayden said. Was I pushing away the possibility of anything good or real? Was I scared of getting hurt again? I pushed the thoughts out of my head and reached into my purse for my cell phone. Maybe it was the conversation with Hayden, or maybe it was too many whiskey sodas, but I impulsively decided I had to see Michael. The phone rang three times and as I was about to hit "end", he picked up.

"Amalia?" he said. "It's after midnight, is everything all right?"

"Yeah, everything's fine. Um, Michael?" I said with a shaky voice. "Is it all right if I come over?"

Chapter 22

Do you love him?

"So this movie we're going to watch, are you sure it's supposed to be good?" Michael asked as he crossed to the couch and handed me an overflowing bowl of popcorn.

I playfully grabbed the bowl from him and scooped a generous amount into my hands.

"Yes," I said, shoveling the snack into my mouth. "It's about a young woman who studies abroad in Brussels, and within a few months her family stops hearing from her and she is presumed to have gone missing."

"All right, Hastings, sounds like a chick flick, but I'll give it a shot." He clicked on the television and then handed me the remote to do the rest.

It was a Friday evening and Michael and I were watching a movie I had gotten from Netflix that morning instead of joining our friends at some club in the Meat Packing District. As we sat on the couch, I couldn't help but notice how comfortable we were with each other. Michael must have noticed the stupid grin on my face, because he stopped eating his popcorn and asked me what I was smiling about.

"Nothing," I said, still smiling. I could feel my face growing redder, the longer he kept his eyes on me. Every time we made eye contact, I felt a swarm of butterflies attack my stomach, tearing their way up into my chest.

"Nothing eh?" he asked while inching closer to me.

I refused to answer and kept my eyes glued to the television. Why did he have to be so adorable?

"Shush, it's starting," I said, trying not to laugh.

I raised the remote control to raise the volume, but Michael snatched it out of my hands.

"Hey!" I shouted, pretending to be outraged. "Give it back!"

"Oh you want this?" he asked as he waved the remote over his head. "Well then come and get it!"

I leaped forward on the couch and fell on top of him, causing both of us to topple over and land on the floor. I grabbed the remote, which had fallen out of Michael's hands on the way down, and claimed victory. Before I could gloat, Michael was on top of me. He hovered over me in a push-up position and looked into my eyes. I dropped the remote and lifted my head up to meet his lips. His eyes locked onto mine and I playfully pushed him away.

"Stop trying to get out of watching this movie," I said as I made my way back onto the couch.

As I hit play on the DVD player, I looked over at Michael and I realized something.

I was screwed.

"So how exactly does it work?" Olivia asked as she leaped over a small rock.

The beginning of February was still extremely cold outside, but in the early afternoon the weather was almost tolerable, so Olivia and I had decided to venture uptown and spend a few hours in Central Park.

"It just works, I guess," I shrugged. "It almost works a little too well. For example, last night he came over and we watched a movie, like a total couple."

Olivia stopped walking and took the opportunity to lean on

a large tree.

"I need to take a break, I'm exhausted," she said as she bent over trying to catch her breath.

"You need to stop smoking," I declared as I planted myself on the tree next to hers.

"I know, I know," she said passively as she waved her hand for emphasis. "Okay, back to you and Michael. Does he sleep over?"

"No, but I've stayed at his place before. He's even made me breakfast." I motioned to her to start walking again.

She let out a heavy sigh and reluctantly started walking. "No roommate?"

"No, he lives alone."

"So you sleep over there and eat meals together. That's so strange. I mean, are you two dating? Is he still with Marge?" Olivia asked, shaking her head.

These were not questions I hadn't asked myself hundreds of times. I shook my head. "I don't know if they're still together, because he never talks about her. He doesn't even have any pictures up in his apartment. You don't think Alex knows about us, do you?"

Olivia stopped and cocked her head to the side. "There's no way he knows. Hell, if you hadn't told me, there's no way I would know. Honestly, the two of you are so good at hiding this affair that if you didn't show me the text messages, I probably would think you made the whole thing up!"

My blood ran cold. Affair. Was I the other woman? A sudden large rush of nausea was followed by a wave of guilt.

"Olivia, this is really bad isn't it?" My hands shook. "I'm doing something really bad. Something kind of slutty."

She put both her hands on my shoulders and pulled me in for a hug.

I gently pushed her back and asked again. "Am I a slut?"

"No." she said calmly. "Of course not, Amalia."

I shook my head and suggested we head back downtown. I felt the sudden urge to be anywhere else. Olivia and I walked in silence until we reached the entrance to the subway.

"Listen, I need to meet someone around here. Are you going to be all right by yourself?" she asked.

"You're meeting someone, eh? Could it be your mystery boyfriend perhaps?" I asked jokingly. "He's not married, right?"

She threw her hands up in the air in mock anger, and then started to laugh. "Yes, Amalia, he's actually a state senator, so keep it quiet." She rolled her eyes.

"Very funny. All right, I'll call you tomorrow." I turned and started to make my way down the stairs.

"Do you love him?" she asked.

The question caught me off guard. I stopped and let out a heavy puff of air. "What?" I asked, although I knew exactly what she was asking.

She took a step closer. "I said, do you love him?"

I didn't know why, but I suddenly felt like I was on a game show and the answer to her questions would either ensure my win or my demise.

"Yes," I said, with no more hesitation.

Of course I loved him. Why else would I put myself through all this aggravation?

"Then you're not a slut," she said with a small grin and a raised eyebrow.

I shook my head and made my way down the stairs. I wanted to go home, draw a bath and pour myself a glass of wine. Or maybe bourbon. I'm not a slut after all. How comforting.

Chapter 23

I just want you to be happy

"Do you want to go to Dos Caminos this Friday?" Cassandra asked, as she examined her freshly painted nails.

I had agreed to meet Cassie when I got out of class for a much-needed mani-pedi. Although I had to admit, since it was the dead of winter, I was more in it for the foot massage than the fresh coat of gloss on my toes. The nail salon we usually went to was packed to the brim, so we stumbled onto a much more secluded, and inexpensive, parlor on the Lower East Side.

"I can't." I looked down into the pool of blue water my feet were currently swimming in. "Friday night is Alex's birthday, and a few of us are going out to Stumble Inn."

Cassandra sighed dramatically. "I can't believe you'd rather go out for that pretentious douche's birthday than come out to dinner with me and the new love of your life, Hayden." She swirled her right foot around in the perfumed water.

I couldn't help but laugh, but quickly changed my expression when I saw she was not joking.

"Cass! Hayden and I had one conversation, and I told you he's not really what I'm looking for right now."

"Unfortunately, my dear, what you're looking for is currently unavailable. I think it's time to broaden your horizons." She gave me an all-knowing look.

I was growing increasingly annoyed by this conversation. I didn't understand why Cassie was so insistent on shoving Hayden down my throat.

"This doesn't have anything to do with Michael. I'm just not ready for a relationship with someone new right now. The pain of Nicholas is still fresh, and I am very confused as to what I want right now. I don't think it would be fair to drag someone new into all of this, excuse the term, drama." I handed the manicurist the bottle of red polish I had picked out.

"I think you just don't want to add any more guys to your number," she said, looking down at her toes.

"What?" I asked, although I had a feeling I knew what she was talking about.

"The number of guys you slept with," she raised an eye-brow. "What was Michael? Number five?"

She was correct. There had been my high-school boyfriend, the guy I thought would become my college friend, my *actual* college boyfriend, Nicholas, and Michael.

"Yup," I snapped. "Number five."

"I'm sorry, Amy." Cassie reached over to my chair and squeezed my arm. "I just want you to be happy."

That phrase was one of my least favorite in the English language, followed closely by "At least". For one, it implied I was unhappy, or worse, I was some sort of project people could take on and transform.

I thought back to my high-school boyfriend, Danny. We had one of those on-again, off-again, relationships that lasted for about three years. It was truly exhausting. I had spent the majority of senior year dragging him around with me to places he didn't want to be. Too naïve at the time to realize this wasn't how relationships were supposed to be, I put up with his aloofness. His wandering eye. His reaction to the biggest night of our adolescent lives, when we lost our virginity to each other. After the deed was done, he kissed me on the forehead and said he had to go home because his mom was making dinner. I asked him if we could talk later, and he assured me he'd be home all night. Two hours later I freaked out   and needed to talk to him. His mom said he had left for the night with his friends about an hour ago. She didn't know what time he'd be back.

Even after that little display of un-affection, I continued to date him for a few more months until we got into a blow-out fight at Cassandra's graduation party. I had caught him openly making fun of the college I was going to (as if Rutgers was a bad school) to some skanky girl who couldn't have been older than fifteen. I knew right then and there that I never wanted to speak to Danny again. And after that night, I never did.

In an attempt to change the subject and stop reliving the past, I asked Cassandra where Bryce was taking her for Valentine's Day.

"Oh, right. Actually, he has to work so he told me he's going to make it up to me one night next week." She pretended to flip through a magazine.

"He has to work?" I asked, eyebrows raised high. "Isn't Valentine's Day this Sunday?"

Cassandra started uncomfortably shifting around in her chair. "Yeah, well sometimes he has to go in on Sundays."

All I could think of to do was nod and smile, although I found it alarming Bryce had to work on Valentine's Day, and wondered if it was a bald lie.

"Well, that's good news for me," I said. "Since I just so happen to be single and available on Sunday, you and I will do something."

Cassandra let out a laugh. "Where are we going to go? All of the restaurants jack up their prices and reservations are made weeks in advance."

"We can go to the movies and see something completely un-romantic, like that new zombie movie that just came out," I said enthusiastically.

I was beginning to feel that persuading Cassie to hang out with me on Sunday might be more for my benefit than hers. Much to my relief, she accepted my offer of "co-patheticness," and agreed a girls' night was just what we needed.

"Should we ask Olivia too?" she asked as we made our way to the dryers.

"No, she's dating someone," I reminded her. "Someone" being the operative word.

"Right!" She plopped down on the stool. "Do we know who this guy is yet? I mean, it's been months!"

"I know," I said, trying not to touch anything with my still-wet fingertips. "I think it's time to do some digging and find out just who this mystery man is."

"We're really doing her a favor. For example, he could be married," she said.

"Or a serial killer," I offered.

"Or worse. He could be from Brooklyn." She laughed.

"She lives in Brooklyn," I said defensively, even though I was laughing now too.

"That's right!" Cassie said. "Oh, poor Olivia. She's doomed."

"Is it just me, or do the three of us all have dysfunctional dating lives?" I asked, still laughing.

Cassandra just nodded. The two of us were laughing so hard, the other patrons turned and looked at us disapprovingly.

"We need to get out of here before we get thrown out," I whispered as I carefully grabbed my purse and led Cassandra out of the salon.

When I got back to my apartment, I was utterly surprised to see Christina and Liz sitting next to each other on the couch, watching television.

"Hey you two," I said dropping my purse onto the table.

"Hey!" Christina said, sounding overly chipper. Liz looked up from the television and gave me a small nod.

"I haven't seen the two of you in weeks. Do you even still live here?" I said jokingly as I removed my heavy winter coat.

I could feel my fingertips and toes begin to thaw as I took a seat next to them on the couch. Liz didn't answer me; she just continued to stare at the television. Christina glanced at her, and quickly jumped in.

"I just figured it was time the three of us all got a chance to spend some time together," Christina said with a nod.

"Oh, absolutely," I lied.

"Great!" she said, a little too loudly. "So let's all watch a movie and order take-out. What do you say?"

A long awkward silence made me feel uncomfortable to be in my own home. Liz lifted her head and finally spoke.

"Fine," she said, as if she was agreeing to something completely arduous, like helping someone move, instead of eating dinner with her two roommates. "But as you know, I'm a vegan. So it has to be from some place I can actually eat from."

Christina gave me a pleading look, as if to say "help me!"

I cleared my throat and said, "I know a few good places we can order from, like Café Blossom."

"All right," said Liz, as she returned her attention to the television.

I glanced over at Christina, who motioned for me to follow her into the kitchen. I grabbed the kettle and started to heat some water, then grabbed a few cookies out of the cabinet.

"Listen, Christina, I'm all for bonding, but what is going on with her?" I asked, reaching for a mug from the top shelf.

"Tim left her," she blurted out.

I spun around at the sound of this news, nearly knocking the kettle right off the burner.

"She showed up at the apartment, and he just broke up with her out of nowhere. He packed all of her stuff and put it in boxes before she even got there. He just left everything on the stoop. He wouldn't even let her come inside!" she said, with alarmingly wide eyes.

155

I was stunned by this information, and a little shaken by how similar it was to mine and Nicholas's break-up. More importantly, I was left to wonder if that meant Liz was going to be living here full time again. I thought back to the last time Liz and I were in a room together for more than a five-minute period, and decided it had to have been the dinner at NYU.

"I can't believe he did that. What an asshole. Did he say why he was breaking up with her?" I asked, with feigned concern.

Christina moved closer to me, her brown eyes so wide they looked as if they were going to pop right out of her tiny pretty head. "He told her he met someone else, and that he wants to marry her," she said dramatically. "What kind of jerk does this to a girl a few days before Valentine's Day?"

I peered out of the kitchen and caught a glimpse at Liz. She looked catatonic, just staring at the television. Upon closer look, her perfectly applied eye make-up had smudged down to her cheekbones; evidence she had been crying, although she would most likely never admit to it. She was dressed in over-sized black sweatpants and a black undershirt, a large contrast from her usual mysterious appearance. Even her fire-red hair looked dirty and frizzy, as if she had been walking through the rain for an hour. I had to admit, she looked like a pathetic mess. I didn't know what to say to Christina, I just shook my head and poured myself a myg of tea. Even though I didn't particularly like Liz, I still felt sorry for her. I knew exactly how she felt – blindsided. As if someone had ripped the relationship rug right out from underneath her, with no warning. Exactly how I felt when Nick left me after our first real fight. I turned back into the kitchen and fumbled through the top drawer, which was stuffed with take-out menus, and pulled out the one for Dojo.

"She likes this place," I said sympathetically. "I think I have a bottle of white wine in the fridge we can drink with dinner. Maybe that'll take the edge off of today's events."

I circled what I wanted, and then handed the menu to Christina.

"I'm going to hop in the shower. Let me know how much I owe you," I said as I walked out of the room.

By the time I got out of the shower, Liz had consumed half of the bottle of Riesling I had stashed in the back of the fridge. Under normal circumstances, I would have gotten angry that she and Christina didn't wait for me until they dove into my liquor, but given the circumstances I forgave them. A few minutes later, the buzzer sounded and Christina went downstairs to retrieve our dinner.

"How much do I owe you?" I said as I wrapped a towel around my soaking-wet hair.

"Don't worry about it," she said waving her hand. "Besides, we totally drank most of your wine. Sorry!"

I looked over at Liz, who had managed to go from catatonically depressed to angry drunk in a matter of twenty minutes.

"Whatever. I'll pay you for your stupid wine," she slurred belligerently, as she took another large gulp.

"Don't be ridiculous! You need it more than I do," I said.

She looked up from her glass and shot back, "What's that supposed to mean?"

I looked over to Christina and mouthed the word "help." She quickly walked over to the coffee table, and raised the brown bag of food over her head.

"Who wants vegetable dumplings?" she offered, in an attempt to diffuse the situation.

"Let me help you with that." I grabbed some paper plates and napkins.

The three of us sat on the couch, drinking cheap wine and eating overpriced, vegan organic Chinese food. It occurred to me this was the first time the three of us had ever shared a meal together. It was kind of nice, even though the circumstances under which it occurred could have been more jovial. Liz looked at me for a moment, and I gave her a small smile. I expected her to smile back, to thank me for trying to make her feel better, or at least for recognizing that I too went through a similar situation not too long ago.

Instead, she said, "Are you done with those spring rolls, Amalia? Or did you plan on finishing the entire plate?"

Chapter 24

I Hate Valentine's Day

I stood shivering outside the movie theatre in Union Square and watched as seemingly everyone in Manhattan was happily engrossed in their Valentine's Day joy. I felt a pang of jealousy as I watched happy couples, holding hands, walk into Max Brenner directly across the street. Not only was that my favorite restaurant, but the very place Nicholas and I had spent Valentine's Day last year. We had come here right after Nick and I exchanged gifts at my apartment. I thought about the shiny red wrapping paper and the homemade card, which honestly looked as if it was fashioned by a fifth-grader. But when I opened the present, I found a beautiful white-gold ring with sapphire stones surrounding a small, slightly impaired, diamond. It was the most beautiful gift I had ever gotten besides the diamond studs my grandmother had given me when I graduated high school.

"I want you to wear this as a daily reminder that one day I am going to get you a real engagement ring. With a much bigger diamond of course," he had said as he slipped the ring on my hand.

My friends all thought the idea was ridiculous, that we were too old to be wearing promise rings, but I thought it was sweet and romantic. So much for that promise.

I was shocked out of my trance as a large gust of freezing cold wind slapped me in the face, causing my hair to fly over my eyes and into my mouth. As usual, Cassandra was running late. I was just about to pull out my phone and text her for the second time, when I saw her getting out of a cab on the corner of 13th and Broadway.

"I know, I'm late. I'm sorry!" she practically sang as she ran over to me.

"It's fine," I said. "I've got the tickets. Let's get inside."

I turned to walk into the theatre, anticipating the warm welcoming air, but quickly realized I was on my own.

"Did I tell you Bryce texted me earlier today?" she said with an oversized grin. She grabbed her phone out of her new purse and shoved it in my face. "He told me to have a wonderful V-Day, and he's thinking of me. Isn't that sweet?"

"Adorable," I said growing more frostbitten. "Can we please go inside now? The movie is going to start in less than ten minutes."

"Yes let's—" she started to say, but stopped mid-sentence.

"Cassandra?" I asked, but she was staring at something across the street. I followed her gaze to the same restaurant I had just been reminiscing over. Standing in front was an unmistakable Bryce.

Bryce, and another woman.

"He…was working," she stammered.

Before I could offer any kind of fabricated solace, Bryce put his arm around the curvy brunette and leaned in for a kiss. The two of them looked cozy together, wrapped in each other's arms in an embrace that lasted for almost a minute. I looked over at Cassandra, but she was gone. I spun around looking for her, and noticed she was halfway across the street, making a beeline for Bryce and the mystery girl.

"Oh no," I said to no one in particular, and made my way across the street, dodging taxis and almost taking out a delivery boy on his bike.

Too late. Cassandra had already made her way over to Bryce, and was tapping him on the shoulder.

"Hello, darling," she said in a sweet and seductive voice.

Bryce turned around and his face went white.

"Um, Cassie, hey," he uttered, with undeniable panic in his voice.

"Who is this?" the mystery girl said.

She had a thick South American accent, possibly Argentine.

"Oh, how rude of me. I'm Cassandra. You know, the girl Bryce has been seeing for the past four months. And you are?" Cassandra said with frightening calmness.

Bryce just stood there with a petrified look on his face. He looked over to me for help, but I just smirked and shook my head at him.

"My name is Ariana," she said, turning to Bryce. "And I have been dating Bryce for two months myself."

This news would have been enough for me to possibly throw a punch, although I'm not sure who would have been on the receiving end.

Cassandra, however, kept her cool. "Wow, you've only been dating for two months and he's already taking you out for Valentine's Day dinner? That's so sweet of him. He never did any of that for me, he just gave me the keys to his apartment." She reached into her purse and pulled out a keychain with about four different keys. "But that was probably just so I could come over for a late-night screw," she said as she fiddled with the key chain.

The other girl and Bryce just stood there as Cassandra tossed Bryce's key up and down, catching it over and over in her right hand.

"You see, Ariana, I really did like Bryce. Hell, maybe I even loved him. But now I see he's nothing more than a lying, cheating douche-bag. So he's all yours, sweetheart. I'm done." She kept her eyes fixed on Bryce the entire time.

"What's that supposed to mean?" He folded his arms in front of his chest.

"It means exactly what it sounds like, asshole." Cassandra smiled wickedly. "Have a nice life."

She tossed the key in the air, but this time let it fall into a sewer drain. I took her by the arm and the two of us walked back across the street to the movie theatre. We walked into the theatre in silence and found seats. After the coming attractions started, she finally spoke.

"Amalia," she said, as she scooped out a handful of popcorn. "I hate Valentine's Day."

Chapter 25

Are you happy?

"Thank God it's almost March," I said through chattering teeth, as I pulled my jacket tighter.

"Not a big fan of the cold?" Michael put his arm around me.

I shook my head. "I think I might need to move to southern California or Florida. Somewhere where it's always warm."

We were sitting on top of the Highline, down in Chelsea. I always thought it was strange to turn an old subway line into a park. We cozied up on a bench somewhere between 35th and 40th, partly because it was a great place to spend the day, but mainly because Chelsea was a neighborhood where we didn't know anyone and could spend time together without getting caught. The constant lying was getting to me. Even though Cassie and Olivia both knew, I was finding it more difficult to keep my cool around Alex. Whenever I was around him lately, he seemed very jumpy. I was starting to think Michael had told him what was going on. I took a sip of my coffee. The hot cup warmed my frozen hands.

"Can you believe the semester's going to be over in less than three months?" I asked, without looking Michael in the eyes.

I found it was easier to get through the rest of my day if I didn't look directly into Michael's eyes. Thankfully, the coffee gave me something to do with my hands.

"You're leaving right after it ends, right?" Michael asked, looking right at me.

"Yup," I took another sip. "I'll be gone practically the entire summer."

A few months ago, I was so excited to leave for this trip, but now I felt like it might not be the best idea.

"You don't sound too excited about it." Michael turned his entire body to face me.

"No, I am," I said quickly. "How could I not be?"

I probably didn't sound too convincing. I wracked my brain for topics to change the subject. "What about you? What are your plans this summer?" I asked.

I instantly wished I hadn't asked about his plans, fearing he would answer with some lavish vacation he and Marge were embarking on. I thought constantly of their relationship and what it must be like. He never spoke an ill word about her, which only made my guilt more consuming.

"I'll actually be starting an internship a week after classes end at Langone Medical Center, downtown," he said as he took the coffee cup out of my hand and pulled me closer.

"One week after? Wow, that's not much of a break," I mumbled nervously.

His arm wound around my waist, as if I didn't have enough goosebumps already. Instead of answering, he just looked at me with a small smile. This time, I couldn't avoid eye contact. Michael brushed the windblown mess of my hair out of my face, and softly kissed me.

I wanted to let him kiss me. I wanted to feel the warm envelopment of his arms wrapped around me. I wanted it so much that I pulled away. I softly pushed him off me, and moved over on the bench, just far enough that our knees were no longer pressing against one another's.

"What's the matter?" he asked.

I couldn't figure out how to explain this feeling. I couldn't find the words to tell him how every time we kissed, I needed two days' worth of recovery to feel like myself again, not like some pathetic love-sick puppy. I looked up and he was staring at me, waiting for me to speak. Waiting for me to explain myself.

Suddenly, I didn't care anymore. An impulsive rush, a sort of word vomit was coming up with no reserve. I blame the fight-or-flight hormones; they're so hard to control. I had to know if he was happy with Marge, or if he was planning on leaving her. I had to know if I meant anything at all to him, or if he was just using me for sex while his girlfriend did God knew what in Arizona.

I whipped around on the bench so I was facing him, nearly knocking my coffee over, but I didn't care. For once, it was time for me to look him in the eyes. My shakiness was gone and I felt strong enough to find out the answer to the question I had been avoiding for months.

"Michael," I started, voice steady and strong. "Are you happy?"

I expected him to question me, to give me one-sided back talk. To say something like "Happy with what?" which would make me angrier and eventually cause me to drop the subject with nothing resolved. But for once, he didn't. For once he actually looked me in the eyes and gave me a straight answer. Unfortunately, the answer was yes.

"I am," he answered softly.

He had a new expression in his eyes, one I had never seen before. A look of pity. That's when I realized, he felt sorry for me.

I stood up, grabbed my purse and coffee cup, and waited the obligatory three seconds for him to try to stop me from walking away. I waited for him to grab me and say, "Don't leave, I need you. I'm only happy when I'm with you, and everything else is facade. I love you!"

He didn't, which made me realize he probably never would.

Fueled by anger and self-loathing, I slowly backed away from him, my eyes still locked on his. "I can't do this anymore."

I walked all the way home.

Chapter 26

What happens to men when they move to Manhattan?

"So that's it?" Cassandra mumbled through a full mouth of mint-chocolate ice cream.

Through all my fury and depression, I still couldn't help but wonder how she ate so much and stayed so thin.

"What do you mean?" I asked, raising an eyebrow. "Would you stick this out? No, I can't. I feel guilty, anxious, pathetic, and to be frank a little slutty. I can't chase him anymore."

I grabbed the tub of Ben and Jerry's out of her hand, and bogarted the rest.

"It's just that… never mind," she said, magically needing to use the restroom at that moment.

"Oh no you don't." I got up to follow her. "What were you going to say, missy?"

Cassandra spun around in the hallway and performed her customary act of crossing her arms and pouting her lips. I stood there, awaiting a lecture.

"I'm just saying, I thought the two of you were going to end up together," she said.

There are things people will say to you in life to make you feel better. This was not one of those things. I knew she was just trying to help, but it sounding condescending.

"I'm sorry, Amy! I don't want you to get hurt, but I didn't think you would give up this easily."

I felt a sudden surge of anger and an overwhelming need to defend myself. "Give up easily?" I said, slowly walking toward her. "Do you have any idea how difficult it was for me to say those words to him? All I want is to be with him!"

Cassandra at this point was flattened against the wall, wide-eyed and panicked. I didn't understand why until I realized I was inches away from her face.

I backed off. "I'm sorry! I'm an asshole."

I put my hands on my face and returned to the living room, where I reluctantly resumed my comfortable position as couch potato. Cassandra rolled her eyes and proceeded to the amenities. As I flipped through the channels, I wondered how I let things get to this point. What were my intentions with all of this? Did I honestly think he would leave his girlfriend for me? The sad truth was, I didn't even know. I stopped on a repeat of *Sex and The City*. It was the episode where all of her friends accidentally missed her birthday dinner and Mr. Big showed up in the end with balloons.

I thought back to my birthday two years ago with Nicholas, and how wonderful my life used to be. I could still smell the melting wax from when it leaked onto the cake because I took too long to make a wish. I could still hear his voice.

"Would you wish for something already!" Nicholas said, hysterically laughing at this point. The candles had been lit for about five minutes, and the wax was starting to hit the frosting. "I don't want to eat birthday candle-flavoured cake!" he joked.

"I can't," I said, not caring about the goofy smile I must have been wearing. "I can't make a wish, because, my love, I have everything I could ever want."

That conversation was one of the best I had ever had. I meant every word. At the time, I didn't think I could ever want or need anything more.

I was slapped back to reality by the sound of Cassandra clunking something heavy down on my coffee table.

"That better be a bottle of vodka," I said without looking up.

"What time is your class tomorrow?" she said, ignoring me and opening a second gallon of ice cream.

"It's at eleven," I uttered mournfully as I remembered the fact that even when you're depressed, life carries on.

"Make sure you look hot," she said.

"Yeah, priorities," I muttered.

"Oh, also, I gave Hayden your phone number."

"I am seriously going to murder you one of these days," I said, too irritated to fight with her.

I reached for my phone, which simultaneously started to vibrate. I scrolled through the list of unread emails and stopped at the most recent one. I read the details; it was dated today, March 7th, and it was from Nicholas.

"You have got to be kidding me," I said, barely moving in my seat.

"What's the problem, dear?"

I couldn't answer her. Instead I sat eerily still and read the three-line email.

Amalia,
Hi, Hope all is well. My sister gave me a sweater of yours she had borrowed, and asked me to get it back to you. What is your mailing address?
-N

Cassandra waved her hand in front of my face and said, "You want to tell me what's going on over there? Or is this a silent stewing sort of thing?"

I couldn't even speak. I was stunned at the amount of nerve Nicholas had, contacting me so bluntly after all this time. I tossed my phone at her, and waited for her to read the email.

I wondered what had happened to Nicholas. He used to be such a sweet guy. What happens to men when they move to Manhattan? It's as if their soul is surgically removed and replaced with dark, hollowed-out indignation the minute the ink dries on their new Upper East Side lease. They forget who they were, and what they used to want, and suddenly only focus on one-night stands and all-night benders in garish hotel bars. This is not what I signed up for when I moved here.

"What the fuck?" Cassie said, giving me a look nothing short of bewilderment. "Why wouldn't his sister just send the sweater back to you herself?"

"I don't know," I shook my head. "But I don't care either. I don't want it back and that's what I'm going to say." I got up and started collecting the dishes. "But I'll say it tomorrow. Right now, I'm going to sleep."

Chapter 27

Last Meal

"If I knew the T.A. was going to be teaching the class today, I would have skipped it," I said to Olivia, who was frantically taking notes.

Although there were still two months left in the semester, people were starting to crack over the thought of finals.

"Have you heard anything from Michael?" Olivia whispered.

"No, not since The Highline. I am doing my best to avoid him. Besides, I have the Nicholas drama to worry about now."

"What are you talking about?" she asked, suddenly concerned.

Olivia was wearing a long string of pearls and a brown sweater dress with lace embroidery on the collar. She looked like one of those American Girl Dolls I would get catalogues for as a child, and way overdressed for class.

"Are you going somewhere after this?" I asked, scanning her outfit.

"Don't change the subject," she shot back, frowning.

"You are, aren't you?" I smiled. "Do you have plans with someone?"

Olivia just looked at me, clearly not amused or willing to back down.

"Fine," I conceded. "Nicholas sent me an email yesterday, claiming to have something of mine, and asked for my mailing address."

"Doesn't he know your address? You dated for a few years."

"I don't know," I said. "The thought had crossed my mind. But I wrote back telling him to keep it."

"Good," she said. I looked up and realized people were leaving; class was over.

"Thank God that's over," I rubbed my temples.

School was becoming an increasingly low priority on my list. I just wanted to get out the moment any class began.

"Are you coming?" I asked, halfway out the door.

"You go ahead. I just have to ask John something," Olivia said, flattening out her dress.

"You call our T.A. John?"

"What do you call him?" she asked innocently.

"Okay fine, just call me later," I said over my shoulder.

The classroom we were in was large, but not exactly auditorium-sized. For some reason, our class was always taught in the dark. An old projector was still set up in the front from when our professor showed us a film on amnesia last week, and the seats were a rustic wood that looked as if it had been exposed to corrosive elements for the past fifty years. It reminded me of a dingy movie theatre I came across once on a family vacation to Danville, Pennsylvania. I had demanded my money back after a loose screw in the chair poked my leg so hard it drew blood. I breathed a sigh of relief that I was done for the day, and opened the heaviest door in academic history. As soon as I turned out of the austere classroom, I spotted Michael and Alex talking. Even across the hallway, his eyes drew my gaze, and immediately my heart sank into my stomach.

Tears began to well up behind my eyes, the kind that burned my throat and made me question whether I'd ever be truly content again. Despite my melancholy, up until his point I hadn't done much crying over Michael. The pain was deeper than that, deeper than simple tears. As if something important had been cut out of me. Befuddled and depressed, I walked back into the classroom, unaware if either of them had seen me.

I slowly made my way to the front of the now-empty classroom, looking for Olivia. I needed someone to calm me down before I walked back outside and was forever known as the chick who cried in grad school. I wiped my eyes, so she wouldn't know I was crying. As much as I needed a friend, I did not relish the thought of anyone seeing me cry. I got closer to where she stood by the podium. I opened my mouth to call out her name, but then I realized she wasn't alone. I couldn't quite make out who she was standing with. I covertly moved closer, being careful not to let my shoes clank on the ceramic tiles. Finally, the figure came into focus. It was our T.A., John. Then I remembered she had told me she needed to ask him a question. They were standing face to face, only a few inches apart. Suddenly, John reached for Olivia, and pulled her in for a hug. I clasped my hand over my mouth in an effort not to gasp. All of a sudden, it became clear; Olivia was sleeping with our T.A.! I slowly backed away, trying my best not to draw attention to myself, and made my way back outside. I darted down the stairs, out onto the street, and made my way to Washington Square Park, where I firmly planted myself on a cold stone bench. I put my head in my hands and rubbed my eyes. Had I really just seen that? If the school knew about this, Olivia could get put on probation. Exasperated, I shook my head and reached in my purse for my copy of Emily Giffin's latest novel. I had to get my mind off this calamity.

While searching for the book, I looked up at the arch. The giant, beautiful white arch at the Fifth Avenue entrance of the park always looked like it was glowing at this time of day. I made a mental note never to stop being in awe at the beauty of New York; at least it was one thing about the city that was consistent.

When I arrived home two hours later, I made a beeline for my bedroom, completely bypassing Christina, who was in the kitchen cooking something that smelled very ethnic. I face-planted onto my bed and took several deep breaths. Compelled to be unconscious and not have to think about Michael or Olivia, I was annoyed when a few moments later I heard a knock on my door.

"Hey," Christina whispered, slowly turning the doorknob.

"Come in," I said, muffled through my pillow.

"Amalia? Are you all right?" She walked closer to my bed. "We're kind of having a roommates' dinner, you in?"

I lifted my head off the pillow just high enough to comply. "Can you just wake me when it's ready please?"

"Sure," she said, quietly closing the door behind her.

The last thing I wanted was to sit through dinner with Liz, who would without question further my bad mood, but I'd promised Christina I would make an effort and I didn't want to rock the boat.

The room was dark, my bed was warm, and just as I was drifting into my nap, my phone began to vibrate. I lifted my face off the pillow to see who it was, but all it said was "Unavailable." My exhaustion beat out curiosity and I let my voicemail pick it up. Thirty seconds later, my phone vibrated again, this time indicating a voice message. Before I could dial to check it, Christina called my name through the door, summoning me to dinner.

Half asleep, I stumbled into the living room, where Christina and Liz were already gathered around the coffee table, pouring themselves each a glass of white wine. Without looking up from her glass, Liz asked me to sit down and make myself comfortable. I looked over at Christina to see if she knew what Liz was going to tell us, but she seemed as unaware as I did.

"I have something to say to the both of you," she said tightly as she topped my glass off.

I reached for the wine, grateful to have a cushion of alcohol for this undoubtedly irritating news.

Liz put down her wine glass and announced, "I'm going to be moving out. I found a place in Astoria with my cousin and next week I'm going to be moving in with her."

Now this was the best news I'd heard all week.

"Next week!" Christina said, genuinely surprised. "Why so soon? I mean, can't you stay a little longer?"

I coughed up a little of my wine, which went down the wrong pipe as a reaction to Christina's attempt to persuade Liz into staying longer. In fact, if it would get Liz out the door sooner, I would gladly help her pack and pay for a cab!

"No, it isn't possible." Liz, let out an exasperated sigh. "I already paid the first month's rent and security deposit, so I'd like to move in there as soon as I can. I'm sorry for the short notice, ladies, but it's just something I have to do, for me."

I sat back on the couch and wondered if Liz ever did anything that wasn't "for her," and then happily thought about how I wouldn't have to ever deal with her again. In an effort to appear supportive, I raised my wine glass and proposed a toast.

"To Liz," I said smiling. "May your new home bring you peace and happiness."

The three of us clinked our glasses together and then we each took a sip. I cut into the baked eggplant Christina had prepared, unknowingly for Liz's last meal, and took a big bite. Things were looking up.

Two pieces of eggplant and four glasses of wine later, I re-stumbled back into my now pitch-dark bedroom and returned to my bed. The activity light was blinking on my phone and I remembered I had a voice message that needed to be checked. Bleary-eyed, I selected the option to listen to my messages and impatiently waited to find out who was yet again disrupting my sleep.

"Amalia, it's Nicholas. I know I am most likely the last person on earth you want to be talking to, but I really need to speak to you. I miss you."

Click.

I looked at my phone, as if it were solely responsible for delivering this message to me, and dropped it onto my rug. I was too tired to feel any sort of urgency, and too tipsy to feel any sort of emotion. I did the only thing I could do. I closed my eyes and immediately fell asleep.

Chapter 28

A David Lynch Movie

The streets of the village had transformed into a scene out of a David Lynch movie. People looked way too happy. The happiness was undoubtedly due to the copious amounts of alcohol people were consuming all day.

To the Irish, this particular holiday commemorates the patron saint of Ireland, Saint Patrick and the arrival of Christianity in Ireland. To New Yorkers, it commemorates green beer, shots of Jameson, and scantily dressed girls wearing what can only be described as sequined cocktail napkins designed to make them resemble sexy leprechauns (if there ever was such a thing).

As I walked out of Red Bamboo, with my takeaway tofu parmigiana in tow, I noticed Alex walking toward me. I tried my best to keep my eyes looking straight ahead, convinced that if I didn't make eye contact with him, he wouldn't see me. No such luck.

"Hastings!" he shouted, darting over toward me.

I lifted my eyes from the pavement and gave him a nod. He was dressed casually, something he hardly ever did. He had on a dark-brown leather jacket, his usual skinny jeans, and oversized, gold-rimmed aviator sunglasses to pull the look together. I looked down and noticed he was carrying a shopping bag from La Perla. Probably for his flavor of the week.

"Whoa, La Perla? Who is that for?" I reached for the bag.

Alex pulled the bag out of my reach and laughed.

"Now come on, Amalia, a gentlemen will never kiss and tell," he said with a small smile.

"Perhaps," I shot back. "I didn't realize I was talking to one."

"Well as much as I love our banter, I wanted to ask you something. I am actually happy I ran into you," he said, placing the shopping bag on the ground. "I'm having a get together at my apartment tonight for St. Patrick's Day and I wanted to invite you."

"Where do you live again?" I asked teasingly. "The South Bronx?"

"Very funny, Hastings. I live on Roosevelt Island. Take the F train from Union Square, and you can't miss it."

I took a step back, glancing once more at his outfit.

"What's with the look?" he asked, suddenly seeming self-conscious.

"Is it by any chance a costume party?" I asked sarcastically.

I was really pushing it with Alex, considering he was friends with Michael and could very easily run back to him and tell him just how nasty I was. I considered this, and then justified that the enjoyment I got out of mocking him was worth the risk.

"What do you mean by that?" he challenged.

"Well," I said looking him up and down, "with the aviators, leather jacket, and skinny jeans, you kind of look like a gay Roy Orbison."

Alex shook his head, grabbed the shopping bag off the ground and tossed it over his shoulder. He was a good-looking guy. If only he wasn't such an arrogant prick all of the time, I wouldn't have to be so hard on him.

"And on that note, I will be seeing you tonight," he said. "Oh, and if you could pick up one of those slutty leprechaun dresses to wear, I would be eternally grateful."

"Never going to happen," I said, turning to walk away.

"Maybe some thigh-highs to match?" he shouted halfway down the street.

Just like that, any feeling of guilt I had over being a bitch to him was gone.

By the time I got to the front door of my apartment, I had three missed calls. One from Olivia, whose calls I had been avoiding since I saw her lip-locked with our T.A., one from Nicholas, whose calls I had been avoiding since he started contacting me again, and one from my mother, whose calls I just avoid.

I was delaying confrontation and acting like a coward. I would have to see Olivia tonight at Alex's place, assuming she was going. I wondered if she would bring John. The thought made me shudder so hard, I could barely turn my key in the door. The moment I did, however, I was immediately taken aback. The apartment was covered with flowers. Not just flowers, sunflowers, which just so happened to be my favorite. I tossed my keys onto the kitchen counter, right next to a ribbon-tied bouquet of sunflowers. I made my way through the hallway into the living room, where a vase of them was decoratively sandwiched on the coffee table between a stack of back issues of Vanity Fair and Christine's Proust collection.

I sat down on the couch, unable to move, and scanned the room solely with my eyes. Flowers bloomed on the windowsill, on the bookshelf – flowers on top of flowers. Who did this? Why would they do this? I felt a sudden overwhelming urge to call the police, as someone had surely broken into my home. Channeling all of my energy, I scrapped the call to the fuzz and made my way into my bedroom, not overlooking the vase on top of the toilet. As I entered my bedroom, sure enough, more flowers greeted me.

I thought back to this morning and decided today really was like a David Lynch movie. Seemingly innocent at first, but an underlying feeling of dread inevitably leads to horror and chaos. There on my pillow, a solo sunflower, most likely staining my linens with its pollen. I picked it up off my bed and held it to my nose. It smelled beautiful, like the distant memory of summer, a season I hadn't seen in what felt like years. For a moment I imagined all of these flowers were from Michael. I imagined he changed his mind, that this was his way of telling me he loved me and that he was leaving Marge. And then I noticed the vase on my desk, with a single beige envelope sticking out on the side. I held it to my chest and closed my eyes. If I prayed, this was a good time to do so. I opened my eyes and read the note.

Amalia,
There are really no words to describe just how foolish I have been, but I'm going to give it a shot. You were (are) the most important thing in my life. I can't apologize enough for the way I treated you, and on your birthday no less!
I am infinitely sorry, and will do anything to get you to speak to me again. Please forgive me. I love you – always and forever.
-Nicholas

I dropped the card on the desk. Something about this felt off. A rush of emotion washed through me that I couldn't pinpoint. Anger? No. Happiness? No. Then I figured it out.

Fear.

The whole Michael debacle had done a great job of distracting me from the pain of Nick leaving. Now, it seemed, he wanted me back. Regardless of whether or not I was going to call Nick, one thing was certain. I had to get all of these flowers out of the apartment. I took a single flower from my bed, pressed it inside one of my biology textbooks and began to purge the rest. I grabbed a black garbage bag from underneath the sink and went to town. By the time I was finished disposing of the evidence – if I didn't see something, I wouldn't have to deal with it – I decided now would be as good a time as any to do a full-blown spring cleaning. I slapped on rubber gloves, armed myself with Clorox, and made my way into the bathroom.

The cleaning frenzy lasted longer than anticipated. By the time I checked the clock, two hours had passed and I had to start getting ready for Alex's party. Snapping off the rubber gloves, I plopped onto the couch, exhausted. Michael would probably be at Alex's apartment, and my day was going to most likely get worse, not better. I rubbed my eyes. How did my life get so complicated? When did I start feeling so sorry for myself all of the time? It was time to start making decisions, to stop sitting back and waiting for life to happen to me. I got up and made my way into the bedroom to change clothes. On the way there, I grabbed my cell phone and scrolled down to my address book. If I was going to this shindig, I was going to need backup.

Chapter 29

Shadows of sobriety

"Oh my God, we're going to die!" Cassandra shouted, aggressively pulling at my arm. "This tram car is going to flip over and fall out of the sky."

"Could you lower your voice?" I said in an elevated whisper. A family stood nearby, with their five-year-old son staring at us, panicked. "It's okay! She's just a little afraid of heights." I smiled politely at the mother, who then proceeded to pick up her child and move to the other side of the tram.

Cassandra and I were on our way to Alex's St. Patrick's Day party, and it was a little bit of a trip to get there. There are two ways to get to Roosevelt Island. The normal way is to take the F train and get off at the Roosevelt Island stop. The other way is to take the overhead tram from 59th street that runs on a cable over the water. It runs about every fifteen minutes and you're only on it for about five or six. This would be a breeze except my good friend Cassandra is petrified of heights, which I'll admit to overlooking when asking her to join me on this excursion.

A few minutes and a few claw marks from Cassie's nails later, we arrived on the other side of the water to the elusive island. Roosevelt Island is a small island in between Manhattan and Queens. It is inhabited by 9,520 people, one of whom happens to be Alex Carlson.

"So, why are we here again?" Cassandra asked, stumbling over her four-inch Louboutins.

"We're making an appearance. Showing Michael, and all the others, that I'm fine," I said with as much gumption as I could muster up. "I'm tired of letting everyone else make decisions for me, Cass. Michael, Nicholas – it's time for me to just live my life the way I want to, and if someone wants to come along for the ride, well then that's great."

"Wow. That's amazing, Amalia, good for you!" Cassandra said as we approached Alex's apartment building. "You totally should have brought Hayden to make Michael jealous."

"Cass, I haven't talked to Hayden since the night we all met," I laughed. "So if you are in fact trying to set us up, you're not doing a very good job."

She stopped walking and smoothed out her green dress. Unlike me, who believes that dressing up like a sexy leprechaun is childish and provocative, Cassandra fully embraced the opportunity to shine.

"Well, whatever. He'll call you eventually," she fluffed up her hair.

"I really don't care," I answered, staring at her outfit.

"I still don't know why you chose to wear jeans," she said, disappointed I didn't join her in this tradition.

"Because I'm fresh out of buckles, and green was never my color. Can we go in now? I'm a little cold."

When we got to apartment 32F, I quickly realized we were the first to arrive. It was 8:00 on the dot, but I should have realized most people wouldn't start to show up until 9:00.

Turning on the charm, Alex immediately took our coats and offered us each a glass of wine. I graciously accepted and took the liberty of giving myself a tour of the place. Alex's apartment was nice, really nice, in fact. I knew he came from family money, but now I could see I didn't know the half of it.

He lived alone in this huge, two-bedroom, two-bath apartment.

The shades in the living room were open, revealing a gorgeous evening view of the Manhattan skyline. The door to the master bedroom was closed, so unfortunately, I couldn't sneak a peek in there. His kitchen was huge; All-Clad cooking ware elegantly suspended from the ceiling. The rest of the kitchen was completed with a dining area you could actually sit down in. Most New Yorkers end up perched on a stool by the counter, or eating on their living-room coffee table; it is quite unheard of to have a dining room. The furniture was brand new, possibly from ABC Carpet or Restoration Hardware. Not a hint of Ikea in the joint. Even the dark-burgundy throw pillows were perfectly placed on the plush beige-colored sectional. The matching burgundy lamps on the end table made me wonder if he had a decorator, or an interior-design team. The rest of the living room was pulled together by a state-of-the-art entertainment system, completed with Denon surround sound. He definitely did not have to be in graduate school. His family clearly had enough money for him to be set for life. I immediately hated him more.

"So what do you think of the digs?" Alex grinned, fighting with the cork on a bottle of white wine.

"I have to admit, you've done well for yourself," I muttered, doing my best to take the acidity out of my voice.

Alex smiled as the sound of the cork popped out of the wine bottle. He reached above him and grabbed three expensive-looking wine goblets.

"So, Amalia, why didn't you dress up?" Alex asked, challenging me.

"I'm not Irish, so I don't usually celebrate the holiday," I said, putting it as simply as I could.

"Yeah, sure, me neither." He poured three glasses of wine. "But don't you want to be a part of it?"

"A part of what?"

He placed the bottle down on the counter top and looked at me through confused eyes.

"Part of the whole scene?" he said, as if it was obvious. "Don't you want to go out and experience New York City?"

"Of course I do," I shot back. "I just don't think thigh-highs and food coloring are that important."

"It's not about the costumes, Amalia. It's about embracing all this city has to offer. It's about feeling like you're a part of something," he declared, unfazed by my defensiveness.

"I don't think I need to dress up and binge-drink in order to prove myself, okay?" I said, hoping to finally prove my point and move on.

"If you say so, Hastings." He took a sip of wine. "I guess you're just not a true New Yorker."

This infuriated me more than I probably should have let it. Being challenged by Alex on my social standing was one thing; hell, he could even tease me about my academics if he really wanted to, but there was no way I was going to let him tell me I wasn't a real New Yorker.

I put my wine glass down and took a step closer to him. "Listen buddy, you have no idea what you're talking about," I started my diatribe, speaking slowly. Measured. "There's more to being a New Yorker than reading *The Village Voice* and getting drunk in SoHo every other night. And not that I have to defend myself to you, but I have lived in New York my whole life and my parents are from Queens. I'm about as New York as it gets. You're the one who moved here from 'Anytown USA' a whopping six months ago. I lived here before the precious Highline ever opened, and I was here when that haberdashery you love so much down in Alphabet City was a crack house. So don't give me speeches about your little *amateur night* holidays and how they somehow reflect your Manhattan-ite status. And don't you *ever* sit here and act like *I'm* not a true New Yorker."

The room fell silent for a brief second, and all I could hear was the dinging of the elevator arriving down the hall.

"Okay, Amalia!" Cassandra twisted her mouth into an

uncomfortable smile. She laughed politely as she pulled on my arm, dragging me over to the couch. "Let's take a seat and get out of Alex's way so he can finish setting up."

I shook my head and followed her. The sound of the door opening stopped my heart and I whipped around hoping to see Michael. I was quickly disappointed. It was only Olivia.

"Hi, Amalia!" She nearly knocked Alex over to give me a hug. "I feel like I haven't seen you in so long."

I had been avoiding Olivia since I saw her with our T.A. I softly hugged her back.

"Hey, Cassandra, how are you?" she asked, giving out another hug.

Olivia seemed to be in a wonderful mood, or maybe she was already drunk. I think I smelled a hint of Crème de Menthe on her breath, or did I imagine that?

An hour later, the apartment was packed, and Olivia was bombed. St. Patrick's Day, New Year's Eve, Independence Day, and even Cinco De Mayo are often referred to as "Amateur Night." It's the few special evenings of the year when people who are usually reserved or light drinkers all year round come out of the shadows of sobriety and use the holiday as an opportunity to go a little crazy.

Make that a lot crazy.

Olivia was currently dancing on the end table that held the beautiful burgundy lamp. Or should I say, used to hold. Olivia kicked it off the table during an interpretive dance set to an LMFAO song. Was he really still playing Party Rock Anthem? A few seconds later, Alex sprinted over to the table in the living room, and grabbed Olivia. He effortlessly flung her over his shoulder and carried her fireman-style into the spare bedroom.

"Well this was fun," Cassandra said and she downed the remainder of her green martini.

It went down easier than the green beer. Or the green potato chips. And was that green bread on the counter, or had Alex just not gotten a Fresh Direct order in time?

"So, I'm going to leave," she grimaced, placing the empty glass on the scene of the crime.

"No, you can't leave yet!" I pleaded. "It's still early, plus I heard there's a shipment of green cupcakes from Georgetown Bakery on their way. Yum!"

Cassandra just shot me her best "are you kidding me" look.

"All right, fine, but I'm going to hang out for another hour or so," I said. "Do you know how to get back?"

"Oh I sure do," she whipped out her cell phone. "Hi, I need a car back to Manhattan, please."

I shook my head and laughed; of course she would never take the tram again. I hugged Cass goodbye and sat down on the couch.

I let out a soft sigh. Pretty much everyone I knew had left, or had to be put to bed. The party still went on around me. People were toasting, and making out in corners. One guy just ran toward the bathroom, odds were to vomit. As I looked around the room at my peers, I thought about how ridiculous it all seemed. I went through this phase in my undergrad years. Now New York City seemed just like college, but with a bigger campus. I took the last sip of my green wine and resolved to call it a night.

"Done already?" Michael asked. I turned around and he took the seat next to me on the couch.

"No, not yet. Fashionably late?" I asked with a small smile. I was happy to see him, but I didn't feel my usual heart pounding excitement. "You missed the show." I raised an eyebrow and pointed to the broken lamp.

"I heard," Michael said, putting his arm around the headrest, which placed his arm somewhat around me. "Alex is in there with her now, holding back her hair."

"Well, that's gentlemanly of him," I scoffed. "He should really get back out here; his pristine apartment is being torn apart."

"The cleaning lady will come in the morning, and it will be as if none of this ever happened." He turned toward me and looked me up and down. "No green?"

"What, my Riesling didn't count?" I said playfully. I shook my head and smiled. "No, I didn't feel the need to partake in the festivities."

"So then why are you here?" he asked.

Why was I here? Was it to run into Michael? I hadn't seen him since our talk on the Highline, and I had to admit, this conversation wasn't a completely comfortable one.

I looked at Michael. He was so gorgeous. Even now, wearing a green button-down with a black sweater over it, he was easily the most handsome guy in the room. But somehow, it wasn't enough anymore.

I thought about everything Michael had put me through this year. Making me feel like he had feelings for me, when he was obviously using me for sex. Keeping the status of his relationship covert, and then spending New Year's Eve with Marge. Not showing up for my birthday after being the one to suggest we all get together. But above all, his dishonesty. His dishonesty to me, to his girlfriend, and even to himself. The truth was, he had no idea what he wanted, and after nearly a year of pining over him, I decided that was no longer my problem.

I looked down at the nearly empty glass in my hand and took a final swig. I placed it on Alex's glass coffee table next to about three more empty wine glasses and a copy of *Gentlemen's Quarterly* and stood up. I was woozy from all the wine, but I was still in a clear enough state to make it to the F train.

"You know what, Michael? Now I'm done," I said. "Have a good night."

Before he could answer, I grabbed my coat and walked out.

Chapter 30

Jersey Girl

Before Michael, before NYU, even before New York City, I was a college student studying at Rutgers University. For four years, New Brunswick, New Jersey was my home, and Harvest Moon on George Street was my local watering hole. Nicholas and I used to spend nearly every Friday night there. It was the best place in town to grab a beer after going to Stuff Yer Face for some stromboli. To this day, Harvest Moon still holds fond memories of my time at Rutgers, which after the year I'd had felt like a lifetime ago. So when Nicholas suggested we meet there Wednesday evening for a drink, my nostalgia got the best of me and I finally caved in. After he flower-bombed my apartment, I started to soften up to the idea of talking to him again. Not necessarily getting back together, just a conversation.

But it was no easy trip to get there. First, in order to get to Harvest Moon, which was in New Jersey, I had to go home to Staten Island to get my car. Now I had two choices. I could go into my house, have a conversation with my parents (or a debriefing, as I like to call it) and answer a thousand questions about school, my love life, and whether or not I'm still carrying around that pepper spray on the subway. Or I could just take the car from in front of the house without saying a word to them. I had the keys with me;

it was completely doable. The only hiccup was that they might assume the car had been stolen and I'd run the risk of giving them both a heart attack – and getting pulled over. I figured I'd chance it and take the car anyway. So on Wednesday afternoon, I began my journey.

Located at the end of the Financial District, or the beginning of Battery Park, however you want to look at it, is the ferry that runs all day and all night for free and goes directly to Staten Island. This sounds convenient in theory, but it is littered with homeless people, drunks, and what I can only assume are "ladies of the night." So, after a short trip on the Staten Island Ferry, which for the record is terrible, I made my way to my parents' house to clandestinely steal my own car.

There it was, just sitting there patiently in the street, awaiting my return home, my 2004 Honda Civic. Blue on the outside, black on the inside, amazing all over. The car was given to me as a birthday present by my father, who insisted I could not possibly drive a used car, as they were often referred to as "death traps." Many make-out sessions were had in this car, along with mini road trips on days Cassandra and I would ditch school. I felt a warm rush of excitement knowing I was going to drive it for the first time in months. I shook off the feeling; I had to focus on my mission at hand. My dad was undoubtedly at work, but my mom's car was in the driveway, so I had to be sneaky. I fumbled in my purse for the keys and accidentally dropped them on the pavement. Before I bent down to pick them up, I saw my mother through the front window.

"Shit!" I whispered, and dropped down to retrieve my keys, and also use a neighboring bush to hide. I crouched into a ball and willed my mother to go back into the other room, away from the front window so I couldn't be spotted. I had officially reached a new point of humiliation.

I felt my phone buzz and reached into my purse to retrieve it. I kept jumping every time my phone went off lately. It was just an email from Express about a sale on skirts. I had hoped it would be something more interesting, but I had enough drama to handle.

A short eternity later, my mother finally left the front room and I seized the opportunity to hijack my own car. I sprinted out from behind my neighbor's bush and smacked into my car. I had forgotten to hit the button to unlock the door, or the remote hadn't worked right. Finally in, nervous about possibly drawing more attention to myself, I started the car and peeled out. It reminded me of a Clint Eastwood movie, or Thelma and Louise, but instead of some great expedition, I was driving to see my ex-boyfriend, who had left me high and dry about five months back. What had become of my life?

Forty minutes after committing Grand Theft Auto on my own car, I had made my way over the Outer-Bridge Crossing, through the New Jersey Turnpike, and onto Route 18. I was just pulling into a parking deck in New Brunswick when my phone went off again. It was Cassandra, texting to see where I was. I had completely forgotten I was supposed to get dinner with her tonight. I grabbed the phone and quickly wrote back that I was sick, and that we could get together tomorrow.

It was official, I was a scum.

I was committing theft – well, not really, the car was mine – lying to my best friend, and spending time with someone who not too long ago had broken my heart. I gave myself a slap *Ow!*, slammed the car door behind me, and made a break for Harvest Moon.

It was a nice day out. The beginning of April and the sun was finally shining. I felt like I hadn't seen it in years; I took it as a sign. When you're in Manhattan, it seems like you never really notice a nice day. The only sign of it is when restaurants open their side doors and allow for outdoor seating. That's about it.

When I got to the front door, Nicholas was already inside sitting at the bar. He looked exactly the same. A rush of nostalgia overwhelmed me. Suddenly, I remembered everything. I remembered the smell of his cologne, Bruce Springsteen's song Jersey Girl playing the first time we kissed, my 150-square-foot dorm room, and lastly how much, at the time, I had loved him.

I was wearing a white and turquoise sundress and a light-grey cardigan over it. I might have been overdressed for a bar, but better overdressed than underdressed. I felt sexy and confident as I entered the bar and made my way over to Nicholas.

"Hey there," I said, trying to come up with something non-committal. I wasn't exactly nervous about seeing him, but I still wanted him to know I was running the show.

"Hello, beautiful." He turned the bar stool toward me to give me a hug.

His confidence caught me off guard. I was expecting a shell of a broken man, or at least something comparable to what I looked like when I wanted him back.

I turned to the bartender and ordered a Jack and Coke. Before I could say another word, Nicholas started in.

"Amalia, I miss you. I have been missing you for the past few months, and I'm sorry," he said, looking at me with his wide, puppy-dog eyes.

I once joked these eyes could take down a small nation. Unfortunately for him, they weren't having their usual effect. The bartender handed me my drink and I took a sip.

"Sorry for what, exactly?" I tossed my hair back. I was acting a little dramatic, but I honestly didn't care. This guy had hurt me, and if he wanted me back he was going to have to work for it. I had gone through enough crap this year to know what I was willing to put up with.

"For everything," he said, now taking my hands in his. "I'm sorry for how I acted at your birthday party. I'm sorry for breaking up with you and for being so cold when I did, and I'm sorry it took me this long to try to get you back."

I studied his face, trying to figure out if he was being genuine. All of the words he was saying sounded perfect, but I still wasn't sure if this was something I wanted to get into again. I had to admit, he looked good. He was wearing better clothes, finer cologne, he even had a new Hugo Boss wallet when he paid the bartender for our drinks; something he rarely did before.

"Well I have to say, your new career agrees with you," I offered him a smile.

"Yeah, I decided to stop waiting around for things at my job to pick up and to just find a new one. I got Clear Channel to let me begin my internship a few months earlier. They actually hired me after me internship was over. I guess I'm doing pretty well. I am actually moving to a new apartment at the end of the month." He took a sip of his gin and tonic.

"What area are you moving to?"

Nicholas had always defended his tiny dingy apartment in Alphabet City; I was surprised he had decided to move out of there. More likely, he had gotten evicted.

"I found an apartment downtown in a building on John Street, off Broadway," he said casually, as if this wasn't at all strange or uncharacteristic.

"Wait just a minute," I said, shaking my head. "You are moving to the Financial District?"

Nicholas let out a small laugh and answered yes.

"The Financial District?" I repeated. "The only people who live there are Wall Street tycoons and the lawyers who work down there – maybe the cast of Suits. You're literally a few blocks away from one of the most touristy areas in the entire city, possibly the country, and you are going to live there! Now, that I would have never expected."

Nicholas was a good sport about my mocking him; he even said he knew it was a bit out of character for him to move there. But he justified it by saying it was much more safe (which it was), and he would be closer to his work.

"Alright, you've convinced me," I shrugged. "Besides, Battery Park is really nice."

"I guess I'll have to take you for a walk by the water front sometime." He reached for my hand.

Maybe with the new clothes, the new job, and the new home, Nicholas had changed. Maybe he had grown up.

The rest of the evening felt just like old times. I told Nicholas what had been going on in my life, leaving the Michael stuff out of it, of course. I told him about school and how I didn't love it as much as I had hoped. He asked if I was thinking about a career change, but I said no. I still felt strongly about wanting to finish graduate school. Nicholas then made a few jokes about our times in college, even retelling a story that involved us driving around all night looking for bottle opener because we didn't think to buy one after a throwing a party in the dorms.

"You'd think that throwing a party and all, you'd remember the one essential item!" he laughed.

"Hey! I remembered the red Solo cups, didn't I?" I was laughing so hard, tears were streaming down my face. I had forgotten how good it felt to laugh. To have fun. Everything was so serious and stressful lately. Maybe this was what I needed.

"Remember our first kiss? Remember Jersey Girl playing in the background?" he asked, while taking a sip of his drink.

"Of course I remember," I said, speaking softer now, my eyes locked on his.

"I think of you every time I hear that song," he uttered. "Because deep down inside, you're secretly a Jersey Girl."

I couldn't help but laugh.

"I think I have to disagree with you there. I think I always was, and will forever be, a city girl," I said, shaking my head.

For a moment, we just stared at each other. It felt comfortable. Familiar.

After a few seconds, I was the first to break the staring contest, and checked my phone for the first time since I sat down. It was nine o'clock already, and if I wanted to get back to my apartment before midnight, I had better leave right now. I jumped out of my seat.

200

"Nicholas, this was fun," I said, gathering my belongings. "It was good to see you, and I'm glad you're doing well. Even though I have to admit I spent a few months there wishing nothing but misery upon you."

Nicholas laughed and grabbed his coat. "Yeah, I probably deserved it. Amalia, I am really glad you agreed to come out here tonight. I really do miss you so much, and I would love nothing more than to give this another shot."

I stood up and gave Nicholas a hug, and told him I'd think about it. I wasn't about to rush back into something, but I at least owed him another shot. We had been together for a long time, and maybe he really was sorry.

"So where are you off to now?" he asked. "Back to the city?"

"Yup," I answered, as we walked out the door. "But first, I have something to return."

Chapter 31

Twenty-four Days

Over the next few days, I began to feel a mixture of confusion and deep self-loathing. Something about my current situation did not seem right. I thought back to how easy my life was in college, and it made me feel foolish for believing it would always be that way. Just one guy, one girl, and no cheating. No subtext or inner monologues. No deep-seated resentment for my ex, or obsessive idealization about someone I never really had.

My head was swimming with anxiety. Should I get back together with Nicholas? We did have a lot of history. Should I have been so quick to tell Michael off? And why was Michael so complacent about not speaking to me for so long? Where was my "Say Anything" moment?

The truth was, I wasn't a lucky person. I didn't have particularly nice things. I didn't have a fancy, high-powered job, and last time I checked my Twitter account, I had exactly twelve followers. One of whom was my mother. I definitely didn't stand out.

I should take that internship I applied for in the fall at a Non-Profit teaching hospital outside of the city. I probably wouldn't make a lot of money. But if I did get in, I should seriously consider moving out of Manhattan. Maybe I wasn't a "city girl," like I declared to Nicholas.

Oh, I know! I'd stay in Brazil. Who'd honestly even notice if I didn't return?

Well, my mother might; she'd have no one to demoralize.

Possibly Nicholas; he'd been calling me non-stop for a week.

Okay. I was feeling sorry for myself. This was going to stop now.

I still couldn't help thinking about Michael. I was like a PTSD patient, everything reminded me of him. He was so perfect. Even after seeing Nicholas, even after telling Michael not to speak to me anymore, he was still invading my thoughts. I'd probably be proposed to later in life, and have moved to the other side of the country living in a quaint little cottage in rural Oregon, and Michael would show up the following day. He'd say something non-committal like, "Do you think we made a mistake?" and it would shake me up, and I'd call off my rustic, backyard wedding. He'd make me doubt my decisions, like he was doing right now.

Was I overreacting? Did I make this into something it wasn't? Was this my fault?

"Here we go. Get it together, girl."

Okay, I was officially talking to myself.

March came and went, and with it any communication I had with him. It was now Saturday, April tenth, exactly twenty-four days since Alex's underwhelming St. Patrick's Day party. Twenty-four days since we'd last spoken. I'd done my best to avoid him in class, showing up a few minutes late, and sneaking in the back. Sitting near the doors allowed for a quick and clandestine exit. I almost ran into him in Union Square last Tuesday, when Olivia spotted him and Alex and wanted to say a quick hello. I told her I suddenly wasn't feeling well and darted into a cab.

I was supposed to see Nicholas tonight. The last two dinners we had since I saw him at Harvest Moon – once at Revel, a trendy restaurant in the Meatpacking District, and once at Serefina, a highly known, and highly priced, Italian place on Madison Avenue – were interesting. Oh shit, tonight I was supposed to see his new apartment. Should I bring him a bottle of wine? I needed to write this stuff down. I couldn't believe he knew about trendy restaurants that I didn't. Did he find this crap in *The Village Voice*? Oh no, absolutely not. He wouldn't be caught dead reading that trash. I really still couldn't believe he lived down in the Financial District.

What a sell-out. What was next, a membership at the SoHo House, and a timeshare in the Hamptons?

Why was I being so critical? What was wrong with me?

I needed a drink.

It was April tenth. That meant I had approximately three more weeks until finals. I couldn't wait until this semester was over. Maybe that was bad; maybe I need a career change.

Maybe I should figure all of this out.

Like where was I? I swear I turned onto 6th Avenue, or was that 9th? Did I walk downtown by accident?

I needed to get to 11th.

Cassandra was going to flip out on me if I was late for lunch, especially after she found out I lied about being sick. I was worried she and Olivia were going to stage an intervention with me this afternoon. That was if I ever made it to The Frying Pan. At least it was a nice day out.

Their speech would be unavoidable. They'd say something like "Amalia, what are you doing? Don't you know Nicholas will only hurt you again? You're not going to give up going to Brazil, are you? You're not moving down to the Financial District, right? Neither of us lives by a six train, and we won't be able to come visit you!"

See, I didn't need to go to lunch. I already knew what they were going to say.

Maybe I'd just cancel.

Shit, I was there.

Chapter 32

Sniff the cork

"I'm coming!" I grabbed my pink terrycloth robe and wrapped it tightly around my freshly-showered self.

The hot shower was a much-needed cleansing after I had gotten severely drenched walking home in the rain from lunch with the girls. Lunch, which had turned into dinner at Coffee Shop, which regretfully turned into drinks at Sidebar on Irving. I hadn't gotten home until nine.

My day was essentially a six-hour-long inquisition. Olivia had asked me a least three times if I was over Michael, and Cassandra at one point grabbed my phone and threatened to delete Nicholas's phone number.

At this point, I wasn't sure what would come of Nicholas and me. After going to his swanky downtown apartment, I started to feel more and more uncomfortable around him. He had gone from living in a dingy walk-up to a doorman building that looked more like a metropolitan hotel than a residential building. He had ordered in instead of cooking, and when he poured me a glass of wine, I could have sworn he had a smirk on his face when I neglected to sniff the cork.

The doorbell rang for the second time, and I glanced at the time on the clock. Who was ringing my bell at 10p.m.? Whoever it was, they were probably looking for Christina. Weren't we all? I hadn't seen her in at least a week. Not at home, and not around the neighborhood. I was seriously considering calling the cops.

There's a strange feeling girls have whenever we hear the phone or doorbell ring. We're always secretly hoping it's the guy we like. Here to profess his undying, unwavering love for us. Standing there with flowers, chocolates – or in true New York City fashion, Cronuts – ready to run away somewhere exotic. I thought about Michael and wondered if he was capable of such romance. Then I imagined Nicholas doing it. Both seemed a little out of character.

My ten-second fantasy got the better of me, and before I could reach the door, the knob slowly turned. The front door made a soft, creaky sound. Panic washed through me.

Crap! I'm going to get stabbed in my apartment, aren't I? And in this tacky Hello Kitty robe too, what a way to go!

I darted into the kitchen and grabbed a butter knife. Of course Liz had taken the paring knives with her when she moved out. I heard the rest of the door swing open, followed by a man's voice.

"Amalia? You home?" said a familiar, soft male voice.

My paranoia was quickly relieved. If this was a criminal, he wasn't a very good one. I put the knife down and walked back toward the door, tightening the belt on my robe that had essentially fallen off in my state of terror.

There in the doorway stood one of the saddest sights I had ever seen. My poor younger brother, drenched from the rain, standing in my doorway with the same overnight bag he had taken on a camping trip we took together when I was nine. The thing had to be older than Justin Bieber. I couldn't tell for sure, but he looked as if he had been crying.

"Aaron, what the hell are you doing here? Are you all right? Quick, get inside and dry off," I said, grabbing the old green bag out of his hands. "What's going on?"

Without saying a word, Aaron slowly walked into the apartment and plopped down on the couch. He looked terrible. I walked over and put my arm around him, and tried to comfort him. My efforts failed, and he just sat there holding his puffy face in his hands. He definitely had been crying.

"Hey, Amalia, good to see you. Listen, can I stay here for a few days?" he asked through soft sobs.

"Um, of course you can," I answered. "Can you please tell me what's going on? I'm worried about you."

Aaron lifted his head out of his hands, and plopped them into his lap. He stared at the floor for a few seconds before answering.

"My girlfriend and I broke up," his eyes immediately filling back up with tears.

I scoured my memory for mention of a girlfriend. Were there any pictures in his room, or anything on Facebook? Perhaps a romantic Tweet? I did notice he was wearing a new shirt over Christmas break; maybe that was a gift from her? I thought back to our weekly emails, and nothing. He had never before mentioned a girlfriend.

"Um, Aaron, what girlfriend?" I asked as non-judgmentally as my voice would allow.

Aaron looked at me, eyes filled with rage and tears. It reminded me of when we were children and he would lose a balloon tied to his wrist.

"Allie!" he said, practically shouting. "Her name is Allie. She was the one."

I didn't know what to say. The idea that my little brother had already found and lost "The One" before graduating college was a little ridiculous to me. Still, he looked terrible and it killed me to see him this way. I thought back to how horrible I felt when Nick broke up with me. If he was feeling half of that pain, I had to take care of him. I grabbed a leftover napkin from yesterday's take-out that I had irresponsibly left on the coffee table along with a cup of soda that had now made a pretty nasty ring in the wood.

"Okay, so tell me what happened with Abby," I said while blotting the tears on his cheeks with the napkin.

"Allie! She cheated on me with a fraternity guy. She claims she was drunk, but that's no excuse. We broke up this morning and I hopped on a bus and came straight here. I couldn't go to Mom and Dad's, and I definitely couldn't stay at school. If I stayed there, I swear I would have beaten that guy's ass." He said, pushing my hands away from his face.

"All right, you have to calm down. You can stay here, it's not a problem. As for beating up that guy, he's not worth it, trust me. And you are right, being drunk is no excuse, even if she was at a fraternity party."

I felt proud of myself, taking my little brother in and giving him advice. I took the decorative pillows off the couch and tossed my brother an extra comforter I stored in the hallway closet. I'm sure Christina wouldn't mind him staying on the couch for the weekend; she was hardly ever home anyway.

By the time I was done fussing, Aaron had calmed down a bit.

"So," I started, trying to find the right words without sounding like I was attacking him. "Why didn't you tell me you had a girl-friend? And also, how long were you two together?"

Aaron let out a heavy sigh. Clearly this was a conversation he was not looking forward to having.

"I didn't tell you because, well, she asked me not to." He looked down at the floor.

"What do you mean?" I said, as I moved away from Aaron and crossed my arms.

"No, don't be offended. It's not just you," he started. "I didn't put it on Facebook or tell any of my friends because she didn't want to make it public. She said it was our relationship and it was nobody's business. I thought it was sweet and sort of romantic. Now I realize it was just bullshit so she could hook up with other guys."

The sad thing was, that was probably exactly why Allie didn't put it on Facebook. The whole scenario kind of reminded me of Cassandra and Bryce. Was nobody in a normal, healthy relationship anymore? Cassandra got screwed over by Bryce, Olivia was in the midst of some secret romance with our Teacher's Assistant, and not to mention the mess I was currently in.

I glanced at the clock. If I wanted to get any sleep before class tomorrow, I had better go now.

"Well, It's getting pretty late, so I am going to hit the hay," I said, patting his knee. "Have a good night, little bro."

I turned off the light and headed out of the living room. Before I could make my way to the bathroom door, Aaron's voice stopped me.

"Hey, Amalia, wait. Can I ask you something?"

"Sure."

"I know it's probably none of my business, I mean especially with what you just found out about me. But, are you back together with Nicholas?"

"Um, no," I said, surprised by the question. "We have been talking and spending time together again, but we certainly have not gotten back together. I mean, I am thinking about it but I still don't know if I can ever really trust him again. But wait, why are you asking me this?"

"Well he IM'd me on GChat the other day and said you guys were back together," he said. "I told him I knew nothing about it and that I didn't want to get involved."

"Interesting," I felt an increase in my blood pressure. This new attitude of Nick's had to stop. Sending a billion flowers to my apartment was one thing, but dragging my brother into this situation was uncalled for. If he wanted me back, talking about our relationship, or lack thereof, to my Aaron, was not the way to go about it.

"Thanks for the heads up, I'll talk to him about that tomorrow."

"Goodnight, sis." Aaron rolled over on his side, and within seconds he was out cold.

I smiled. It reminded me of how innocent he was when he was a child. Now he had experienced his first heartbreak, and it most certainly wouldn't be his last. I made a mental note to remind him never to move to Manhattan.

I pulled the blanket around him and whispered, "Goodnight, bro."

Chapter 33

Bro's

I took another sip of my Jack and Coke as I waited for Nicholas to arrive, who was already fifteen minutes late. When he suggested meeting at P.J. Clarks, I was a little confused. It wasn't by either of our apartments and it was usually inhabited by families during the day and smarmy financial types in the evening. I assumed he was held up by the train and took out my phone to see if I had any missed calls from him. I reminded myself to talk to him about what my brother had said about him saying we were back together on GChat.

Instead, my phone displayed a text message from that guy Hayden. All it said was, "Hey! How are you?" but that was too much for me to deal with at the moment.

My attention shifted to the entrance when a small crowd of obnoxiously laughing guys made their way into the bar.

"Idiots," I whispered and returned to my phone.

I was confused when one of the rowdy guys call my name. I look up and realized that was my rowdy guy. That was Nicholas, and he brought friends.

"Amalia!" he waved, making his way over to me.

"Hey, Nick," I said. "You made it."

"Yeah, sorry babe, work ran a little late," he said through a snicker.

I looked over to his friends, who were also snickering. I made a mental note of their appearance. Cheap, unfitted suits. Sharp, short haircuts. And the faintest hint of Armani cologne. It reminded me of the Bro's and Secretary Hoe's parties the local fraternity house used to throw at Rutgers.

"Aren't you going to introduce me to your friends?" I asked, trying to stay calm. I could feel my lips twist into a grimace and I pretended to cough to erase it.

"Oh yeah, sure," he said turning to face them. "Guys, this is Amalia. Amalia, this is Jim, Dave, and Andrew."

"Nice to meet you all," I said, giving a small wave.

They waved back and then scurried over to an open table near the window.

"I didn't know you were bringing your friends with you," I said quietly to Nicholas. "Are these guys you work with?"

"Yeah they work on the same floor is me. Man, Andrew is hilarious! Just wait until he gets a few beers in him. They were bored and asked to tag along," he said. "Are you mad?"

I was mad, but I didn't want to rock the boat, considering we had just started talking again. It could, after all, be an honest mistake.

"No, of course not. I just wish you had mentioned it because I would have asked Cassandra to come too," I headed to the table.

"Ah, I'm glad I didn't tell you then," he muttered under his breath.

"What did you say?" I asked frowning at him.

"Nothing, babe. You know Cassandra and I just don't always get along."

"Okay, fair enough. But I could have maybe asked Aaron. He's staying with me and feels a little lonely."

"I don't really want some kid hanging around with us, Amalia," he said, looking around the room.

"He's only a few years younger than us," I offered, wondering why he was being so difficult.

"Yeah, well, it's just not my thing." He shrugged.

"Yeah, well your bro's don't really seem like my cup of tea either, but that doesn't mean I'm not going to give them a chance," I snapped.

Nicholas stared at me, and then looked over to his friends to make sure they didn't hear my comment.

"Let's just try to have a nice night," he said walking away from me to join them at their table.

"Yeah," I said with a sarcastic flair. "I'll try"

Chapter 34

We belong together

"What's wrong?" Nicholas asked, taking a sip of bourbon. "You don't like your food?"

I was sitting at a table in a restaurant I had never heard of, in a part of town I had never been to before. In fact, I wasn't even sure if I was on the West or East side of Manhattan. It was some new, up-and-coming neighborhood that would undoubtedly have some catchy acronym as its name within the next few months. I never really did like the name "DUMBO" for that area of Brooklyn under the Manhattan Bridge.

Normally I would be excited to try new things and go new places, but tonight I just wasn't in the mood. In fact, Nicholas had brought me here essentially against my will. I had suggested going out to eat at Blue Smoke, a moderately sized BBQ joint in the Flat Iron district that we frequented back when we were happy. My attempts to reclaim normalcy were shot down, and now I was overwhelmed and underdressed in this fancy French restaurant. Or was it Turkish? Either way, I just wanted a turkey burger, not a deep-fried lamp chop smothered in balsamic-flavored mustard.

I was still trying to forget our evening at P.J. Clarks. Last night had gone from bad to worse when two more of his friends from work showed up. This time, the friends were girls. Which I usually

218

wouldn't care about, but when corporate casual obviously translates to high-end hooker, I get a little pissed.

"Not really," I answered, pushing my food around on my plate. "It's not really something I would normally order."

I summoned the waiter over and hoped he'd be able to suggest an alternative.

"Excuse me," I said as politely as possible. "I don't eat lamb and the menu wasn't in English. Is there something else I can order? Do you have any eggplant or maybe something with mushrooms in it?"

The waiter stared at me blankly before finally answering with, "We have veal. Would you like that instead?"

I shook my head no, and diverted my attention back to the almost empty glass of Riesling in front of me.

"That was a little rude," Nicholas said, shaking his head.

"Excuse me?" I asked, not politely. I raised my eyebrows and crossed my arms in front of my chest. "How exactly was I the rude one in this situation?"

There are only a few things that will get me very angry very quickly. One of them is provoking me while I'm hungry.

"You were a little rude to the waiter, and not to mention embarrassing to me," Nicholas answered curtly.

"Oh really? I was rude?" I started. "Well I happen to think it's pretty rude to invite someone to a restaurant where they not only feel uncomfortable, but also have no choices on the menu they can eat. What happened to our casual night out? I'm the one who's embarrassed wearing jeans in this place."

"Keep your voice down." Nicholas was looking around the room as if I was making a scene. Maybe I was, but at this point, I really didn't care.

"Hey, let me ask you something," I said dryly, leaning in closer to him now. "Did you tell Aaron we were back together?"

Nicholas put down his knife and fork. He looked nervous, which was rare for his new composed disposition.

"Um, no I don't think so," he said picking his utensils back up.

"Why do you ask?"

I watched as he took a big bite of his medium-rare steak. I secretly hoped he would drop some on his Hugo Boss button-down shirt he just took the tags off of this morning. I bet if I looked in the dumpster behind his building, I'd find enough Jane's Addiction T-Shirts to clothe half the homeless in New York.

"Aaron said something to me about it the other night. As you know, he's staying in my apartment this weekend."

"Well, I don't know what your brother's talkin' about, babe. I haven't spoken to him in at least two months," he said with a smirk.

"Really," I asked coldly. "So you didn't talk to him a few days ago?"

"Nope, haven't heard from him. The guy's a little weird anyway, I don't talk to him much," he answered.

"A little weird? What's that supposed to mean?" I cocked my head to the side, growing angrier by the second.

Nicholas began looking around the room nervously. Or maybe he was just scanning the joint for people he knew. He had slipped the host in the front a twenty-dollar bill so we wouldn't have endure the forty-five-minute wait. I wasn't having fun anymore. Now was as good a time as ever to tell him what I really thought about his new attitude.

"Are you calling my brother a liar?"

Normally I wouldn't get this angry this quickly, but a part of me was looking for a reason to fight with him.

Nicholas gave me a look. His eyes were narrowed and sharp. Long gone were the days of his soft looks and genuine personality. "Amalia, you're seriously crazy. I'm not having this conversation with you," he said through gritted teeth.

"Oh, no?" I asked, even more sassy than before.

Nicholas looked at me through the same narrowed eyes. "What's your problem tonight?"

"You're my problem," I said sharply as I pointed my finger at him. "Don't go blabbing to my brother that we're back together and then lie about it to my face, number one. Number two, you may have traded hemp for Hugo, but that doesn't mean you get to act like you're better than me."

Nicholas's face turned bright red, and he fumbled for his drink. Realizing it was empty, he slammed the glass down on the table, causing the neighboring patrons to point and whisper. A part of me felt severely satisfied I had gotten him to break.

I shook my head at Nicholas, disgusted at what he had turned into. "I know it's just an act. I know that you feel like you have to impress everyone now that you have this new job. But truth be told, I liked you a lot better when you were living on Ramen and boxed wine," I said, trying to keep an even tone. "At least then you acted like a decent guy."

I reached into my purse and Nick watched in horror as I threw two twenty-dollar bills on the table to cover my portion. I pushed my chair out, almost knocking it over. Someone said "Watch it!" as I spun around and headed to the door.

Nicholas chased after me and we got as far as the next street corner before he could finally figure out what to say. Either way it was useless. I was done.

"Amalia, you're making a mistake," he called to me, slightly out of breath. "We're meant to be together."

He caught up to me just as I turned around and looked him right in the eyes. I had loved this boy so much, for so long. Now, he was a stranger to me. Another cookie-cutter Manhattan-ite. The absolute last thing I wanted in my life. Getting back together with him had been a mistake. It was an act of desperation out of deference to past memories and nostalgia. Those feelings would never be recreated and I had to move on. I looked at him one last time, and I think I heard the theme music to "The Way We Were" playing in the background. Or was I just imagining that?

"No, Nicholas. We're not," I said, letting a hint of sadness come through in my voice. "I don't *belong* with anyone."

Chapter 35

You knew what this was

I checked my watch for what had to be the third time in five minutes, but there was no need. Our T.A., or should I say, *Olivia's* T.A., was giving up-to-the-minute updates of how much time we had left to finish.

Only ten minutes left until this abhorrent semester was over. Now if I could just remember the third bone in the middle ear. Okay, it was the malleus, incus, and the, err something. In retrospect, I should have studied more for this exam. To make matters worse, I arrived five minutes late to class, and the only available seat was directly in back of Michael. Every few minutes, I would take the opportunity to stare at the back of his head. He needed a haircut; it was probably the first time I ever noticed something about him that wasn't perfect. I smiled at the realization. If I could only remember that third damn bone.

"Stapedius!" I said in a loud whisper.

I felt a light shove from behind me, followed by a whispered "Hush!" I slowly looked over my right shoulder to see no other than Alex. He gave me a small nod, and then went back to finishing his work.

I glanced down at my watch once again just as our T.A. called, "Time's up!" Well ain't that for timing?

Slamming my blue test booklet shut, I shook my entire desk, knocking over my pens and water bottle.

"So how did you do?" Alex asked with a huge grin on his face.

A part of me wanted to lie and seem overconfident with my work, but all I could muster up was a soft grunt. But I didn't care. I couldn't wait to get out of this classroom and forget this semester ever happened.

"That good, eh?" he called out to me, as I walked away.

After retrieving my belongings from the floor, I pushed my way through the harem of students; the classroom was never quite as full as when we had an exam. There were people in the classroom who I had literally never seen before. On the way out, I saw a few of them wipe away tears, and a few of them just dead-pan as if they'd been molested during the exam.

I slammed the door behind me, a proverbial "Screw You" to the school. I was then greeted by the sun, which felt particularly bright after being cooped up in the dimly lit auditorium for the past three hours. It was the kind of feeling you get after seeing a matinée at the theatre, except without the enjoyment of being entertained and eating seven-dollar popcorn.

I stormed across Washington Square Park, and headed down 5th Avenue, making a beeline for the subway, when I heard a male voice call my name.

"What is it?" I snapped, expecting Alex to be there when I turned around.

"Oh, I'm sorry. Did I scare you?" answered Michael, taking the brunt of my frustration.

"No, I'm sorry, I thought you were Alex. I am not in the mood to hear one of his one-liners right now," I explained. "But listen, I am going to just head home and I'll talk to you later."

I made it about two feet before Michael called out, "You ran out kind of fast and I wanted to make sure you were all right."

I don't know why, but this stuck out to me. Was I all right? For some reason, coming from Michael, it seemed like the most condescending question in the world. Kind of like when your boss at McDonalds asks you if you're all right after you've mopped the floors.

I took a step toward him.

"You wanted to make sure that I am all right? Seriously?" I asked, venom in my voice.

"Um, yeah?" he asked, taking a step back.

I pressed my hands against my eyes and rubbed them slightly. "Really? Well let's re-cap, shall we? In the past year I got dumped by my boyfriend who then tried to get back together with me only after he turned into the biggest douche-bag in New York, I got jerked around by you for a good six months or so, and now thanks to my complete lack of sleep and studying I probably failed that class. So no, Michael, I most certainly am not all right. But thank you for your bullshit platitudes, I really appreciate them."

He just stood there, looking stunned. It was the first time I'd really ever challenged him, or called him out on how he was treating me. It was clear by his expression he was not expecting that.

"I jerked you around?" he whispered, just loud enough for me to hear. "And how exactly did I do that?"

My blood pressure hit the roof. I had never felt such deep anger before. That someone so blatantly could take advantage of me, and not own up to it. Someone I trusted. Someone I called a friend.

"You led me on, treating me like I was someone you cared about when all you really wanted was sex. You tricked me into thinking we could be more," I said coldly. "I had genuine feelings for you, and you were utterly aware of it. I was vulnerable after my break up with Nicholas and you took advantage of it."

I felt a little nervous saying all of this. After this conversation, I could possibly lose him as a friend forever. But then again, did I really ever have him? Had I been fooling myself this entire time, wishing it could be something more? As I looked at Michael, I couldn't help feeling extreme sadness. His dark eyes were glued on mine, only reminding me of all the intimate times we had shared.

225

I stood completely still, anxiously awaiting his answer. Hoping it was something resembling an apology.

"Amalia," he finally spoke. "You knew what this was."

I waited for the pain. Waited patiently for the overwhelming, all-consuming pain that would undoubtedly flood through my chest.

I waited, and I waited a little longer. But it never came.

I slowly shook my head and turned my back to Michael. The subway no longer looked appealing to me, so I walked the rest of the way home. The whole time waiting for the hurt to kick in, but it never came. I felt nothing. Utterly numb, unaware of any damage that has just been done to me, to my self-esteem, or to any future relationships I may have. I felt nothing. Sadly, it was the best I had felt in a long time.

Chapter 36

All my best, Christina

"Are you sure you have to leave tomorrow?" Cassandra asked, doing her best puppy-dog eyes.

It had been a week since my last encounter with Michael, and I had done a surprisingly good job keeping him out of my mind and focusing on my trip to Brazil. Tomorrow's flight was at 6a.m. Pretty standard for international flights.

"Yes, Cassie," I answered, mockingly. "I'm completely sure the flight is for tomorrow, hence the reason half my closet is spread across the bedroom floor. You're supposed to be helping me pack, remember?"

"Well I can't, Amalia," she said, bordering on whining. "It's just too sad. What am I supposed to do without you this summer?"

"Don't you have a job?" I stood up, and stared over the messy pile of clothing on my floor. This was not something I should have left for the last minute.

"Need any help, sis?" said Aaron, peeking around the door hinge into my bedroom.

Aaron's presence had been a huge calming effect on me this past week. After his big breakup with what's her name, we had a long heart-to-heart. His semester was almost over, so after his last final, I asked him to come back to the city and stay with me until I left. I felt closer to him than I had in years.

"Yes, Aaron. I actually do need some help," I motioned to Cassandra, who was propped up by three pillows, sitting on my bed and reading *People* magazine. "See Cassie? Some people are actually helping me pack."

She kept her cavalier demeanor as she flipped the pages and muttered, "Whatever."

I picked up a blue and gray tank top I remembered buying on a vacation to Boston I took with Nicholas. I waited for the usual overwhelming wave of nostalgia. I braced myself for the feeling of longing, of regret, of believing I made the wrong choice cutting him off. But just like the pain for Michael, it never came. Relieved, I shrugged and tossed the shirt in the trash can by my bed.

"So, any big summer plans, Aaron?"

"Well, now that you brought it up, I actually got a paid internship here in the city," he said, grinning like a fool.

"What! Where, when, how?" I shouted. I felt like jumping up and down for joy, but I composed myself to set a more mature example. "I'm so excited for you. Where are you going to live?"

"Easy there, sis!" he laughed. "I got a small studio apartment up on the West Side. I don't know if I could do the whole room-mate thing. And the internship is at Merrill Lynch. I'm going to be shadowing a financial analyst and learning the ropes of finance. I got it through one of my business professors, after acing his final."

"You hear that, Cassie? Aaron's going to be in the city this summer too. Maybe you can show him around? Get him acquainted with everything? You definitely won't be bored."

This got Cassandra's attention. She bit her bottom lip, which was shellacked with bright-coral lip-gloss, and tossed the magazine on the bed. "All right, little Hastings. I will take you under my wing and show you around. Consider me your cruise director," she said with a smirk. Cassandra gave me a small smile and I smiled back. I was going to miss her.

"You're a good friend, Cassie," I said, blinking away tears.

She walked over to me and gave me a hug. The sound of her heels on the hardwood floor made me laugh away my tears.

"Don't abandon me for some sexy Spanish-speaking guy down there," she mumbled, not letting go. "You better come home, no matter how good the weather is."

"They actually speak Portuguese in Brazil. Why does no one know this?" I laughed.

"Whatever," she said, breaking away from me and sitting on the bed again.

"I hate to interrupt this powwow, but I just found this note for you stuck on the fridge," Aaron said, handing me a piece of loose-leaf paper.

I unfolded the paper and read it out loud.

Amalia,

I've really enjoyed living with you and getting to know you over the past year. I wanted to say goodbye to you properly before you headed to the airport, but I already left myself late last night. I didn't want to wake you, so I left you this note. I won't be returning to Manhattan. I have moved to Cincinnati to begin a new job, and a new life for myself. Don't worry, I paid the landlord my portion of the rent till the end of the month.

I hope you have a wonderful time in Brazil, and you find what you're looking for.

All my best,
Christina

I folded the note back up and put it in my pocket. Something about what Christina said when she wrote "I hope you find what you're looking for," really stuck out with me.

"Well I guess that answers the question, 'Where's Christina?'" Cassandra said.

"I guess," I answered softly. "She didn't even take her couch."

It was a sad realization that I would never see Christina again. She had been good roommate. But that's the difference between a good roommate and a good friend. A good roommate might respect your privacy, but a good friend would never leave without saying goodbye.

Just as I finished putting the last article of clothing into my suitcase, an urgent knocking began on the door.

"That must be Olivia with the wine!" Cassandra clapped her hands and jumped off the bed. "Let the going-away party begin!"

Cassandra darted to the door, but her voice filled with disappointment when she swung it open. "You're not Olivia," she said. "And you obviously don't have any wine, so if you don't mind, we are having a small going-away party for Amalia."

In my bedroom, I made eye contact with Aaron.

"What the hell is going on?" he asked.

"No clue," I sighed. "Let's go see."

"Amalia!" Alex said. "Um, hey. Listen, have you seen Olivia? She told me earlier today she would be here around this time. I need to talk to her."

"Why do you need to talk to Olivia? And why are you at my apartment?" I asked genuinely annoyed. "Seriously guys, I need to pack."

"I'm sorry to interrupt your packing, I know you're leaving tomorrow," Alex said, almost sounding sincere.

"Alex, thank you for stopping by to say goodbye to me or whatever it is you're doing here, but I really need to finish up here."

"Please, Amalia, I really need to stay. Just until Olivia gets here and then I will leave you alone." He looked worried. His normal olive-toned skin had taken on a color more resembling day-old milk. His hair was a mess and it hadn't been raining. I noticed big black circles under his eyes, as if he had been up all night. Or possibly crying.

I took a step closer to his and examined his face more closely. "Alex, are you all right?"

"Excuse me?" Aaron said, making his way up the door. "Um, who's Olivia?"

Just as I opened my mouth to answer, Alex beat to me to it, and said something none of us expected.

"She's my girlfriend."

Chapter 37

Will you stay?

"What the fuck?" I uttered, stunned and still standing in the hallway.

Did Alex just say what I think he did? Had he and Olivia been together this whole time and none of us knew? And why was she hugging Jason in secret?

"We've been dating since the beginning of the semester," said Olivia, who had suddenly materialized outside my doorway.

I looked at her and then looked back at Alex. They were caught red-handed, and clearly had no contingency plan.

"How long have you been standing there? Never mind, this is way too much for me to handle right now," I said, turning back toward my bedroom. "Thank God I am leaving tomorrow."

"Amalia, I'm sorry I didn't tell you," Olivia looked very upset. Like Alex, she had dark circles under her eyes. Her usual pin-straight hair was thrown into a messy bun. "Please don't walk away."

"Look, you can explain later, Olivia. I really need to talk to you now," said Alex, desperation in his voice. "I am really sorry about earlier. You know I love you."

"Wait a second. The two of you are in love?" I shrieked.

The two of them just stood there and looked at me.

"Well actually, this is the first time he's ever said it," said Olivia with her eyes locked on Alex. "But yeah, we are in love. I love you too, Alex."

I shook my head and thought if I shook hard enough I would wake up from this insane dream I was having.

"But you better never hurt me like you did the other day ever again. Understood?" Olivia said with authority in her voice.

"Olivia, I won't. I swear!" Alex said putting his arms around her and giving her a kiss. "Forgive me?"

"Hurt you?" I turned to Alex. "What did you do to her? I'll kill you."

"Don't worry about it, Amalia," Olivia answered for Alex. "It's under control."

This entire situation was bizarre to me. Not only were Olivia and Alex dating, not only were they "in love," but it seemed Olivia wore the pants in the relationship. Watching Alex get bitched around by a girl was the best thing I had seen all year.

"Okay, but wait a second, Olivia," I shook my head, still extremely confused. "I thought you were dating John?"

Now it was Olivia's turn to look confused.

"Um, John who?" she asked.

"Hello!" I said. "Our T.A.! I saw you two after class one day hugging. You were alone and it was dark, so I guess I just assumed you two were together."

Alex quickly looked toward Olivia.

"No! I'm not with John, at all." She crinkled her face into a grimace. "He's gay."

"Really?" Alex and I both said in unison.

"Yes, he's gay," Olivia answered, growing annoyed with the conversation. "I was hugging him because he's been going through a difficult time with his family. They haven't been as supportive as they should be."

"Well, I guess that explains it then," I muttered, a little disappointed. I had been really oblivious to what was going on with my friend this semester.

"I'm sorry we didn't tell you, I just felt it was best if no one got involved in our relationship," Olivia shrugged. "Alex wanted to tell people, but I didn't want the drama to get in the way of my first year of graduate school."

"Mission accomplished," I said under my breath. She shot me another look and I shook my head and gave her a hug. "It's okay Olivia, I forgive you for keeping me in the dark."

I really needed a break from this city. I turned around and looked at Cassandra, who was practically in tears from laughing so hard. I couldn't blame her; the whole thing was pretty ridiculous. After the initial shock of everything was over, Aaron introduced himself to Alex and Olivia and we all had a few minutes to catch our breath and talk.

A little while later, Olivia and Alex completely patched things up, wished me a safe trip, and headed out together. A few minutes after them, Cassandra and Aaron left my apartment too. The two of them were going to grab dinner, and I felt relieved that Aaron would have a friend in the city while I was gone.

I took a look around my bedroom, then the living room, and finally the kitchen. My apartment was empty. Really empty. Besides my bed, the only piece of furniture left behind was Christina's couch. It finally occurred to me that after I left tomorrow, no one would live here anymore. A pang of nostalgia and sadness filled me. It made me think about Nicholas bringing me soup when I was sick, about Cassandra and me talking about life and our choices, and I even thought about my first night with Michael. Even though I had these memories, and most of them were even good ones, I was resolved that I needed a change.

I had arranged for movers to come by after I left to take my bed and the rest of my clothes, and put them into storage for me. I didn't know where I would put them after I returned. Even when I got back from Brazil, there was no way I was coming back to this apartment.

236

When I heard the buzzer go off, I walked toward it slowly, taking the opportunity for a final look around to see if anything else had to be packed. Even without asking, a part of me knew who it was. Still, I was a little surprised when I opened the door a few minutes later, and saw Michael standing there.

"Hi," he said, holding a bouquet of white roses in his hand.

"What are those for?"

"They're for you." He looked sheepish.

"Michael, what are you doing here?" I ignored the flowers. "I have had enough visitors for today and honestly it's late and I have a flight tomorrow morning."

"I'm here because I'm an idiot." He looked into my eyes.

"You're here because you're an idiot?"

"Look, you were right. I wasn't treating you fairly, and with someone who I consider a friend, I really messed up," he let out a long sigh. "I'm sorry you got caught up in the middle of me figuring things out with Marge, and hell, with myself. I'm just not who you think I am."

This was the first time he had ever faced the reality that he had been cheating on his girlfriend. Well, at the least the first time he had ever brought it up with me. He tried handing me the flowers, but I still wouldn't take them.

"Michael, I am glad you came here to apologize. I really am," I said. "But, I'm not really sure what you want me to say to all of this. I mean, it's been about nine months already. Nine months of me lying to people and feeling sorry for myself, and I can't do that anymore. I really care about you, but I wanted more. I can't go back to just being your mistress and hope that one day you'll leave her for me. It's demeaning."

Michael stood there for a second, and took all of this information in. I was proud of myself; I was getting better at saying my feelings. I was so over being passive aggressive.

"Marge and I broke up," he said suddenly.

"Why?" I wasn't sure what I was hoping for, but I was interested as to why they broke up.

"Because we weren't right together."

"Fair enough," I offered, slightly disappointed by the answer. "When did this happen?"

"Three days ago."

I nodded, taking all of this information in. They had literally just broken up the other day. I finally walked out of the doorway we had been standing in for about ten minutes, and sat down on the living room couch, the last remaining piece of furniture in there. Michael followed and sat next to me.

"This day just keeps getting weirder." I put my head in my hands.

Michael placed the roses on the couch and immediately took my hands in his. He brushed the hair off my face and softly kissed me. I tried to move away from him, but he kept his hand on my back.

"What do you want, Michael?" I said softly. He was right up against me. I could smell his skin, his aftershave, his hair. Myriad feelings suddenly came rushing back to me, churning and mixing, the good and the bad. "Honestly, why are you here?"

"I'm here because I want you to stay," he said, looking directly into my eyes. "I know that's a selfish thing to say, but I had to say it. I'm not with Marge anymore, and I'm not saying I want to jump into another relationship right this second, but I don't want you in another country right now either. Maybe we can try and work something out?"

This was a lot to take in.

"Just so I'm clear on this, you're saying you don't want me to leave? You don't want me to go on my trip, you want me to stay here with you?" I said, still trying to wrap my head around this whole proposal.

"I want you to stay, yes. Stay and help me figure this all out."

"Help you figure out what you want. Right?"

I was asking a lot of questions, but I had to know exactly what Michael was expecting from me. And I had to know exactly what to expect from him. I didn't want to be unsure or confused by anything surrounding the two of us anymore.

"Yes, Amalia. That's what I am asking from you," he said softly. "Stay here, with me, and help me figure things out. I care about you."

I was taken aback from this statement. I had wanted Michael for so long. When we first started up, I would have done anything to be with him. I looked into his eyes, ran my fingers through his soft brown hair, and lightly brushed his lips with mine.

"I care about you too, Michael." I nuzzled under his chin.

"So then, what do you say?" he asked, still holding onto both of my hands. "Will you stay?"

Chapter 38

Chase

I hadn't traveled much in my life. In fact, the first time I ever got on a plane was when I was fifteen. I took a family trip to Disney World, and standing under the giant globe in Epcot Center was the closest I ever got to a landmark until I lived in Manhattan. But that globe was nothing compared to the *Cristo Redentor* statue that watched over Rio. The sight of the giant effigy on the mountaintop sent chills down my spine and reassured me I had made the right choice. For the next few months, I was in for something really special.

The harsh truth was, Hayden was right. If you are supposed to be with someone, you won't have to chase them. And although I did appreciate Michael's apology, and even felt happy he had finally broken up with Marge, it wasn't enough anymore. I couldn't stay there and help him figure things out. I knew what I wanted out of our relationship – hell, out of my own life. Staying and being a proverbial contestant with the possibility of winning a relationship with him wasn't good enough for me. Waiting for him to decide would have been a step backward. He was right about something, though. He needed time to figure things out. But he needed that time alone, and if we were meant to be, he'd be there when I returned.

After grabbing a stick of gum to fight the landing pressure, I dropped my purse onto the floor and kicked it under the seat in front of me. The flight attendants came around for the final time to collect any trash, and reminded us to pull our seats completely upright. Excitement and happiness filled me; I had no regrets. I stared out the window one last time and couldn't help but smile as our pilot proudly announced, *"Senhoras e Senhores, bem-vindo ao Rio."*

Printed by RR Donnelley at Glasgow, UK